BEETHOVEN IN PARADISE

Also by Barbara O'Connor

Me and Rupert Goody

BARBARA O'CONNOR

Beethoven in Paradise

A Sunburst Book

FARRAR, STRAUS AND GIROUX

SUMMERTIME, words and music by George Gershwin, DuBose and
Dorothy Heyward, and Ira Gershwin
© 1935 (Renewed 1962) George Gershwin Music, Ira Gershwin Music and DuBose
and Dorothy Heyward Memorial Fund
All rights administered by WB Music Corp.
All Rights Reserved   Used by Permission
WARNER BROS. PUBLICATIONS U.S. INC., Miami, FL. 33014

HOW GREAT THOU ART by Stuart K. Hine
Copyright © 1953 S. K. Hine. Assigned to Manna Music, Inc., 35255 Brooten Road,
Pacific City, OR 97135. Renewed 1981. All Rights Reserved. Used by Permission.
(ASCAP)

The Library of Congress has catalogued the hardcover edition as follows:
O'Connor, Barbara.
    Beethoven in Paradise / Barbara O'Connor. — 1st ed.
        p.   cm. — (Frances Foster Books)
    Summary: Martin longs to be a musician, and with the encourage-
ment of two very different friends, he eventually is able to defy his
mean-hearted father and accept himself and the talent within him.
    ISBN 0-374-30666-4
    [1. Self-acceptance—Fiction. 2. Fathers and sons—Fiction.
3. Music—Fiction. 4. Friendship—Fiction.] I. Title. II. Series.
PZ7.0217Be   1997
[Fic]—dc20   96-17289

For Pooch

I would like to thank the following people
for helping a story turn into a book:
Leslie Guccione, for her generous spirit and helping hand;
Ann Reit, for sharing her time and advice and for
helping me find my wonderful agent;
my wonderful agent, Barbara Markowitz,
for her faith and enthusiasm;
my editors, Frances Foster and Elizabeth Mikesell,
for their vision and wisdom;
my writers' group, for saying all the right things;
my research assistant, Ann, for being my best bud;
the real-life Martin, for his musical soul that inspired this story;
and Willy and Grady, for being so patient when
I was lost in Paradise.

BEETHOVEN IN PARADISE

One

MARTIN DUCKED AS his baseball glove hit the wall. He kept his gaze on the spot where it landed.

"Martin, sometimes I swear you try to make me look like a fool," his father said in that too-calm voice that gave Martin the creeps. "You trying to make me a laughingstock?"

Martin tried to force down the lump in his throat. A tune started in his head.

"You gonna answer me? Look at me when I'm talking to you." Ed Pittman picked up the glove and put it on. "I was embarrassed to call you my son. You let every pitch sail right past you. Missed every ball at the plate, missed every ball in the outfield. Like I never showed you nothing." He slammed his fist into the glove. "There was T. J. Owens barely making an error, and he don't even have a daddy."

Martin stayed put and stayed quiet. Silence made his father mad, but answers made him madder. Martin let the tune grow and tried not to hum out loud.

"You ever practice?" His father slammed his fist into the glove again. "You ever once work this leather like it was meant?" He threw it back at Martin's feet. "Feels like the day I bought it. This sorry glove's got more dust from your closet than dirt from the ball field. I'da given my back teeth for a decent glove and a daddy who'd teach me the game." Mr. Pittman paced back and forth across the trailer floor. "T.J. and the others are out in the field every free minute. Where's my son? Listening to music with a loony woman old enough to be his mamma."

Martin scratched at the dried mud on the knees of his baseball uniform. He tried to let the tune in his head drown out his father's words.

". . . like some damn sissy-britches out there . . ."

Martin made up words to his tune. "I ain't listening to you," he sang.

". . . all your time with that fat fruitcake Wylene . . ."

"I don't hear you," Martin hummed.

". . . think I don't know about that damn music . . ."

Martin's tune stopped when his baseball glove landed in his lap with a thud.

"I got no problem just up and leaving this place, so don't go getting too damn cozy, you hear?" his father said.

Martin traced patterns in the cracked Formica countertop with the tip of his finger, starting and stopping in time to the tune that filled his head. What was his daddy talking about? Why had he moved from baseball to Wylene? Was his daddy mad at him or Wylene or just everyone in general?

"Go away," Martin sang in his head and traced with his finger. "Go away. Go away. Go away."

The screen door slammed. The car started with a roar. Gravel spewed. The tires squealed when the car turned onto the highway. Martin listened to the car race farther and farther away and fade into silence. He had forgotten his mother was in the room until she stirred slightly on the couch. She looked like a dog that had just been beat for the pure meanness of it. He knew it was his fault—and he felt guilty.

"I'm sorry, Mamma" was all he could think of to say.

She looked at Martin with sad dog eyes. "Ain't nothing to be sorry for."

"I guess I just ain't never going to be any good at baseball."

Doris Pittman came over to where Martin was sitting on the barstool. She pulled his head down to her chest and stroked his hair. She smelled like talcum powder. He listened to her heart beating in time with his own, then he sat up and kissed her on the cheek. The corners of her mouth turned up into a tiny smile, and Martin felt better. Most of the time, it seemed to Martin that all the bad days of her life showed on her face, so lined and drawn. Her lips puckered up and twitched at the corners, like they were just busting to let loose with something. Sometimes Martin thought she was living a secret life somewhere in her head. He worried that maybe that secret life didn't include him.

Once he had found a wrinkled photograph in the bottom of her sewing basket. Eight children were lined up like stairsteps in front of a church. The one on the end, the smallest one, was his mother. Martin recognized her tilted-up chin and her skinny bowlegs. She clutched a Bible with both white-gloved hands and squinted at the camera from under long, straggly bangs. Martin had been fascinated by that picture and for the longest time couldn't figure out why. Then one day it came to him. That little girl's face had a peaceful smile the likes of which he had never seen on his mother.

"I'll go get the paper," he said, heading for the door. He'd have to go to the Six Mile Cafe to get the *Piedmont Times*. That was a couple of miles there and back. But that was okay with him. He had a couple of miles' worth of thinking to do.

The breeze felt good on his face as he headed toward the main road. His cowlick stuck straight up on top of his head and waved in the breeze like a banner as he walked. When he heard the *chinga-chinga* of a bicycle bell behind him, he turned to see Terry Lynn Scoggins riding toward him. The handlebars of her bike wobbled as she struggled to keep her balance on the dirt and gravel road. Finally she tipped, then jumped right up and brushed the dirt off her already skinned-up knees.

"Where you going?" she asked.

"Into town to get the paper. Where you going?" Martin picked her bike up and held it steady for her.

"I ain't allowed to go nowhere." She climbed on her bike and wobbled off.

When Martin passed under the big sign that arched over the entrance to the trailer park, he walked backwards for a ways, looking up at it. WELCOME TO PARADISE, it read. Only one problem with that sign. It was facing the wrong direction. Seemed like most of the time Paradise was on the outside of that trailer park. He turned around and headed toward town.

With each step that led him farther away from Paradise, Martin felt lighter. His long, skinny legs took big, bouncy steps. Pretty soon he was practically floating with the freedom of it. Sometimes when Martin walked he was so lost in a tune he could step right over a dead possum without skipping a beat. But today he took the time to admire the splashes of pink-and-white dogwood along the road, gaze at the blue, cloudless sky, and enjoy the smell of new-mown grass. Before he realized it, he was thinking. Thinking about what a puzzle people were most of the time. Thinking about how come his father was so mad all the time. How come Wylene was so sad all the time. Martin was beginning to think he'd never figure people out. About the only thing Martin knew for sure right now was that a couple of miles' worth of thinking didn't bring a couple of miles' worth of answers.

Two

"WYLENE LUNDSFORD IS a grown woman, Martin. If she can't go by herself, that's her problem. It ain't your problem—and it sure as heck ain't mine."

Martin jabbed his fork into his cold scrambled eggs. "I just don't see why Hazeline has to come today," he said.

His mother didn't look up from the frying pan. Bacon grease spit and splattered the wall behind the stove. "Because she's your grandmamma and today is Sunday and Hazeline always comes on Sunday." She pushed the hair out of her eyes with the back of her hand and looked at Martin. "Besides, your daddy'd have a fit. You know he don't want you going to that concert."

Martin leaned across the kitchen counter, tipping the stool forward. "Why not?" he said.

His mother opened her mouth to say something, then snapped it shut and sighed. She took the bacon out of the pan. Crisp, just the way his father liked it. Martin had seen many a too-limp piece of bacon hit the wall with a greasy splat.

Martin let the stool fall back sharply onto all four legs. "Come on, Mamma. Just this once? Wylene don't want to go alone."

"Drop the subject, Martin, before your daddy wakes up and raises h-e-double-l. You hear me?"

Martin pushed the screen door open so hard it banged against the side of the trailer, then slammed shut with another bang. He sat down on the front steps and hugged his knees. Wylene would be mighty disappointed. She'd been talking about the John C. Calhoun High School orchestra concert for months. How they'd been practicing a medley of show tunes from all fifty states. How she'd only heard "Oklahoma!" and couldn't wait to hear the others. But there was no way she'd go alone. Wylene went to work at the Hav-a-Hanky plant on first shift, came home at exactly three-thirty, and stayed put until it was time to go to work again. Unless it was Thursday, when she went to Jay's Superette, or Sunday, when she went to Belle Shoals Baptist Church. Wylene needed life to be predictable.

Martin stood up and shoved his hands in his pockets as he headed up the narrow road that curved back and forth, up and down, through Paradise Trailer Park. He might as well get it over with. Little tornadoes of reddish dust swirled around his sneakers and settled into the cuffs of his jeans. He wasn't more than halfway when the tune of "Oklahoma!" set itself in his head. He walked in time to the song, his thin, straight hair bouncing with every step.

He looked up at the canopy of trees that shaded him from the noontime sun. All the other trailer parks Martin had lived in had been bare. Just wide-open sky above dry, cracking dirt. Hot as all get out in summer. Cold and uninviting in winter. The trailers had been lined up in perfect rows, one beside the other, each one's front door looking out at the stained and rusty back of the trailer next to it. But here in Paradise, the trailers were scattered every which way, nestled among big, shady trees that dropped acorns and hickory nuts with loud pings onto the metal rooftops below. Since the day his family had moved here nearly a year ago, Martin had loved the cool, damp feel of Paradise.

The walk to Wylene's trailer was uphill and nearly clear to the entrance at Six Mile Highway. He wished it were farther. The tune in his head kept his feet moving as he neared the Owenses' double-wide.

"Hey, Pitts," someone called.

Martin looked down at the road and kept walking.

"Hey, Armpit, you going to see your fat girlfriend?"

Martin heard the sound of bare feet slap-slapping on the dirt road behind him. He didn't have to turn around to know it was Riley Owens.

"You deaf or something?" Riley asked, falling into step.

Martin stopped. He didn't want Riley following him all the way to Wylene's.

"You talking to me?" Martin grinned. He had a habit of grinning when he was uncomfortable. Some people thought he was cocky as a rooster when he grinned like that at the wrong times. But on the inside, he was nervous as a hen.

"Who you think I'm talking to, Armpit?" Riley narrowed his eyes and stuck his face close. Martin returned the glare with a cool gaze from half-closed eyes. He could smell chewing tobacco and see little drops of sweat on Riley's slightly fuzzy upper lip.

"I'm taking a walk," Martin said.

"How come you walk so much?"

Martin grinned wider. In his mind he said, "To get away from jerks like you." Out loud he said, "To get where I'm going." But neither of those reasons was the whole truth. Martin also walked so he could listen to the music in his head. Hum it. Clap to it. Even sing some if he wanted to. He'd covered a lot of miles listening to music.

"You have a nice walk, then, Armpit." Riley slapped Martin on the shoulder and jogged back toward his trailer.

Martin's stomach settled into a happy calm. He had enough on his mind right now without adding Riley Owens to the picture. He set his pace to the tune of "Oklahoma!" again. Before he'd even gotten to the curve in the road that led to Wylene's, Martin heard the music echoing out of her shiny silver trailer like a bee in a garbage can. "What a Friend We Have in Jesus" twanged from the open windows.

Martin walked up the orderly brick path that led to Wylene's front steps. She had real steps, not just boards on cinder blocks like most everyone else. A blue plastic birdbath stood out front. Martin had never, not once, seen a bird in that birdbath, but Wylene always kept clean water in it. Beside the birdbath was a plastic hen, followed by a row of little plastic chicks, pecking with their plastic beaks at the dirt. BB guns had long since filled each chick with tiny holes.

On either side of her front door, marigolds grew out of old tires painted white. In the middle of one, a windmill whirligig stood motionless, waiting patiently for a ripple of a breeze to set it in motion. Martin stamped his feet on the HOME SWEET HOME mat, sending puffs of dust into the air. "Tonight at Shady Rest Baptist Church . . ." came from the radio inside.

Wylene hummed on her way to the door. When her eyes met Martin's, her smile drooped. Martin's tune vanished.

"You're not going, are you," Wylene said.

Martin stared at his feet. One shoelace was untied. He fought the urge to stoop to tie it.

"I knew it. I just knew it," Wylene snapped. The tears were already running down her plump cheeks. She turned and walked back inside, pulling her quilted bathrobe around her, bedroom slippers flapping, curlers bobbing.

Martin followed her into the darkness of the trailer. "I

can't," he said. "Hazeline's coming." He ran his fingers through his hair, trying to smooth the cowlick on top.

"Then why'd you tell me you were going? Martin, I was counting on you. I been looking forward to this since Christmas." Wylene sniffed and stuck her lower lip out.

Martin looked down at the green-and-gold linoleum and shifted his weight from one foot to the other.

"I know," he said. "I guess I just didn't think about it being a Sunday and all."

"Well, I guess you didn't." Wylene wiped her red nose with a balled-up tissue.

Martin didn't know what to say next, so he didn't say anything. He sat at the dinette set that divided the kitchen from the tiny living room and caught a glimpse of his reflection in the spotless microwave. His cowlick stuck straight up on top of his head. He pushed it down. Wylene's parakeet pecked at a bell in his cage by the window. A car drove by too fast, sending clouds of dust and sprays of gravel through the trailer park. Someone yelled, "Slow down, you idiot!"

Wylene sat on the velvet couch and stared down at her hands, twisting the damp tissue into little ropes. Her fingers were fat and dimpled, like a baby's.

"I'm sorry, Wylene," Martin said. "I wanted to go as much as you did."

"Then why don't you?"

" 'Cause my mom says I can't."

" 'Cause of that mean-hearted daddy of yours is why. Won't let you go to something as simple as a high-school concert." She stuffed the tissue into her pocket and shuffled into the kitchen. "Hazeline wouldn't care and you know it," she added, opening and shutting cupboard doors, straightening cans of soup, lining up juice glasses.

"Sunny and mild today," said the man on the radio. Ping, ping went the parakeet bell. "M-a-a-a-rtin," his mother called from trailer number 12.

"I got to go," Martin said.

As he walked down the neat brick path, he picked up the beat of the song again.

Wylene's screen door opened behind him. " 'Oklahoma!'—right?" she called. Martin turned and smiled, but Wylene had already disappeared inside.

Three

MARTIN HUMMED, TAPPING a tune with the toe of his sneaker, breathing in the sweet smell of honeysuckle. He patted his shirt pocket to make sure his harmonica was there and craned his neck to watch for Hazeline's big, blue Studebaker. His father's mother lived fifteen miles away in Greenville and came every Sunday to take Martin to the Prince of Wales all-you-can-eat buffet at the Howard Johnson's out on Walhalla Highway. His stomach growled just thinking about the slabs of roast beef, mounds of mashed potatoes, and towers of Jell-O salad.

Taking Martin to the Prince of Wales buffet was about the only thing Hazeline could think of to do with a grandson. Martin was twelve years old, but Hazeline still hadn't got used to being a grandmother.

"Don't ever call me that again," she had snapped at three-year-old Martin when he called her Grandmamma.

"My name is Hazeline," she had said. "Hazeline. You got that?" Then she had scooped him up in her hard, skinny arms and carried him into the house for banana pudding.

Finally Martin heard the crunch of gravel as Hazeline's car pulled up. He ran out to the road to meet her.

"Hey," Hazeline called and flicked a cigarette out of the car window. She turned to gather her bags from the seat beside her. Hazeline wouldn't look like Hazeline without a bag or two hanging from the crook of her arm. Anything was liable to be stuffed in those bags: the Sunday comics, a box of raisins, garden gloves, nail polish, a deck of cards, binoculars.

Martin had found his harmonica in one of Hazeline's bags. It lay there at the bottom of that bag so silver and shiny he just couldn't stop his hand from reaching in and taking it. He had gone into the woods behind the trailer to play it and couldn't make himself give it back. When his father found it, Martin had gotten the buckle end of a belt across his backside. But that belt was the good news compared to having to tell Hazeline what he'd done. Hazeline had looked at him for a long time, so quiet it nearly killed him. Then, calm as anything, she had said, "Well, you just better put that thing to good use, then, you hear me?" And that was all.

Now Martin waited as Hazeline pushed the car door shut with her foot. "You ready?" she asked. "I'm starving, ain't you?" She looked Martin up and down, then shook her head and wiped a smudge off his cheek. "I swear, Martin, you hadn't got enough meat on you to choke a chicken. What you need is some grease in that stomach of yours. Let me give this to your mamma and we'll get going. Look here, ain't these the cutest things?" She took two framed pictures out of one of her bags. Puppies pulling clothes off a clothesline. Kittens tangled up in yarn.

"I found these," she said. "Right on top of Earl Ketchum's trash can. Don't that beat all?"

Before Martin could answer, Hazeline had disappeared into the trailer. The faint smell of whiskey hovered in the air where she'd been just seconds before. By the time Martin got inside, Hazeline was already pulling on window shades, letting them fly up with a snap.

"It's like a damn tomb in here, Doris," she was saying. "Where's Ed? Church?" She laughed at her joke, the too-loud cackle of a laugh that Martin loved.

"Hi, Hazeline," Martin's mother said, not looking up from the *TV Guide* in her lap. "Martin's gotta be back by three for baseball practice."

Martin's insides squeezed up, making a hard ball in the pit of his stomach. He felt Hazeline's eyes on him.

"Let's go," he said, heading for the door.

They had turned onto the main highway and were halfway to Howard Johnson's before either one of them said a word. It was Hazeline who broke the silence. "So, your daddy still making you play baseball?"

"Yeah."

"How come?"

Martin shrugged. "I don't know. I reckon he just likes baseball."

There were a number of things Martin wasn't very good at, and lying was one of them. His face turned red, and sometimes he got a twitch in his left eye.

Hazeline laughed. Smoke chugged out of her mouth like smoke signals in a cartoon Western.

"Just likes baseball, does he?" She looked at Martin out of the corner of her eye. "Martin, you keep forgetting I've known Ed Pittman since he was eating mashed peas and peeing in his diapers. He likes baseball about as much as he likes working—and you and I both know how much he likes working."

"He's working now," Martin said. "He's been at Furniture City since before Thanksgiving." Why did he have this sudden urge to defend his father?

"You're changing the subject," Hazeline said. She lit another cigarette with the stub of the first one. "We were talking about baseball."

Martin sank into the seat and put his feet on the dashboard. He stared out the side window.

"He says all boys play baseball," Martin said.

Hazeline let a little "pfff" squeeze out between her lips. "He sure is good at writin' the Rule Book of Life, ain't he? Hell, the only thing I remember him ever hitting with a baseball bat was your uncle Vernon." Hazeline cackled, and her cigarette wobbled up and down in the corner of her mouth. She squinted as the smoke trailed up in front of her face.

"You ever tried to tell him what you think about baseball?" she asked.

"About a million times."

Hadn't he tried to tell his father he didn't really want to play ball?

"Maybe you need some help getting your point across," Hazeline said. "I'm an expert on that subject if you ever want some lessons." She winked at Martin.

He took the harmonica out of his pocket and played a no-name tune to change the subject.

"Okay," said Hazeline, "I can take a hint."

Martin played whatever tune came to his head and stared out the window at the kudzu-covered fields. The big leaves of the kudzu vine seemed to gobble up everything in the South Carolina countryside. Martin had been told it grew a foot a day. He didn't know if that was true or not, but he had seen it swallow up mailboxes, trees, even whole barns.

"Make me laugh," Hazeline said suddenly.

This was a game they'd been playing since Martin was little and first found that harmonica.

Martin started playing "Take Me Out to the Ball Game."

Hazeline laughed so hard she started coughing and pounded the steering wheel. When she'd recovered, she said, "Now make me cry."

Without so much as a pause, Martin switched to "I'm So Lonesome I Could Cry." The notes drifted out slowly, sadly. Martin closed his eyes and let the music circle around him and take him away. The slippery vinyl car seat disappeared right out from under him and he floated into a calm nothingness. When the song was over, he kept the harmonica at his mouth for a few minutes till the spell was broken, bringing him back to reality. The smoke-filled car. The billboards and telephone poles along the highway. He looked at Hazeline. Tears quivered in the corners of her eyes until she blinked, sending them rolling slowly down her brown, leathery cheeks.

"You're getting too good at this game," she said.

"At least I'm good at something."

Hazeline punched him playfully. "Aw, now, you're good at lots of things," she said.

"Name three."

"Okay." Hazeline puffed on her cigarette. "Playing that harmonica, making grilled cheese sandwiches, and getting crabby old Hazeline to laugh once in a while."

Martin laughed. "You ain't crabby," he said. "Least not all the time," he added, tucking his harmonica back into his shirt pocket.

Hazeline turned the big Studebaker into the parking lot of Howard Johnson's and stubbed her cigarette out in the ashtray. "Let's go put some meat on them bones," she said, poking Martin in the ribs.

Martin followed her across the parking lot. The tune of "Oklahoma!" was swirling around in his head again, and Martin set his pace to it. "Hey, crabby," he called to Hazeline, "wait for me!"

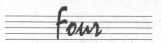

Four

MARTIN DIDN'T SEE Wylene for four days. She'd been working second shift, from three in the afternoon until eleven at night. Martin knew how much she hated it when they were short-handed at the plant and she had to work second shift. Now she was back on first shift and pulling into the trailer park just as Martin got home from school.

He was pretty sure she was still going to be upset about missing the concert. Wylene could hang on to a bad feeling for a mighty long time. The minute he saw her get out of the car, he knew he had been right. Her mouth was set tight and turned down at the corners. Her eyes darted around, not looking at him.

Martin set a smile on his face and walked over to her car. "Want to play Chinese checkers?" he said.

"No, thank you." She lifted a grocery bag out of the trunk. Martin picked up a bag and followed her into the trailer.

"Might be a thunderstorm tonight," he said, lining up soda cans neatly in the refrigerator.

"That so?"

"Reckon we could use some rain."

Wylene glanced at his shoes. They didn't look dirty to him, but he took them off anyway. Speckles of sand fell out onto the floor.

Wylene sorted the groceries in silence. Canned goods together. Boxes together.

"Mind if I put a tape on?" Martin asked.

"Suit yourself." She arranged the boxes by height in the cupboard.

"Got any requests?"

"Whatever."

Martin looked through the tapes. Schubert Symphony No. 9. *Salute to Hollywood.* Vivaldi Violin Concertos. At last he found it. Beethoven Piano Sonatas.

He put the tape on, then settled into his favorite spot on the floor, his back against the couch. He watched Wylene out of the corner of his eye. Her face was set in a determined frown. As the notes filled the trailer, her face began to soften and the edges of her mouth curled up into the tiniest bit of a smile.

Martin slumped into a heap of relief and grinned up at her.

"Mr. Beethoven does it again," he said.

Wylene chuckled. "You're a hard person to stay mad at, Martin Pittman." She sat on the couch, dabbing at the perspiration on her forehead and neck. Her red hair was damp and frizzy around her face.

Martin could always count on Beethoven to bring Wylene around. After all, it was Beethoven who had brought them together in the first place. It had taken about a hundred times of walking by Wylene's trailer before she had done more than give a quick, you'd-miss-it-if-you-blinked wave at Martin. Then one day music like he had never heard before drifted out of her front door.

"I like that music," he'd called to her.

Wylene had looked up from her weeding and stared at him. "You like Beethoven?"

"I reckon I do and never knew it till now," he'd answered with a grin. And that had done it: opened the door a tiny crack.

Now the two of them sat in silence, listening to the music, nodding their heads with the rhythm.

"It just seems impossible that Beethoven was deaf, don't it?" Wylene said.

Martin nodded.

"I mean, can you even imagine not being able to hear and still making up such beautiful music?" Wylene continued.

Martin closed his eyes and listened, trying to imagine.

"You know," Wylene said, "they say Beethoven used to saw the legs off his pianos so he could feel the vibrations of his music through the floor."

Just then a car drove by, horn honking, music blaring from the open windows.

Wylene grunted as she pushed herself up off the couch. "That Riley Owens don't know the meaning of the words 'peace and quiet.' " She pushed the front door shut on her way into the kitchen.

"Want a ham biscuit?" she called to Martin.

"Sure." Wylene made the best biscuits of anybody he knew, including his mother. If Wylene ever got up the nerve to come to a Paradise potluck supper, his mother would lose her title as the best biscuit maker in the county. Until that happened, which would be about two weeks from never, Martin was the only one who knew Wylene's hidden talent.

She set a plate of ham biscuits on the coffee table and dropped back down on the couch, fanning herself with a freckled hand.

"Why you reckon I'm so sad all the time?" she asked suddenly.

Martin took a bite and thought carefully about that unexpected question.

"I mean, I got my health," she continued. "I got a nice home, a nice job."

Martin nodded and chewed. He couldn't argue with the health and home part, but he wasn't so sure about the nice job part. Eight hours a day, five days a week, inspecting handkerchiefs, throwing the bad ones into the discard bin and sending the good ones on down the conveyor belt and into the folding machine, didn't sound like much of a job to him, but he was glad Wylene liked it.

"You know what I like most about you, Martin?" she asked.

Martin's mind raced, searching for possible answers. Before he could find one, she continued.

"I like that you're so comfortable being you."

Now that was something he never would've thought of. "I guess I ain't got much choice in the matter," he said. "I mean, who else am I gonna be?"

"No." Wylene waved her hand at him impatiently. "I don't mean you could be somebody else. I just mean you never want to be somebody else."

"Who else would I want to be?"

"Oh, never mind," Wylene snapped. She picked at a thread on the cushion of the couch. Her parakeet chirped and scattered seed onto the floor.

"Dern it, Pudgie, I just swept in here." She went to the kitchen and came back with a broom.

Martin was still thinking about what she had said. "Sometimes I wish I could pitch like T.J.," he said. "Or flirt with girls like Riley."

"But you never want to be T.J. or Riley." Wylene swept birdseed out the front door.

"I'd have to be some kind of idiot to want that," Martin said. "Riley's about as nice as a possum with rabies, and T.J.'s nice but he ain't too lucky—he got Riley for a brother. Who in the world would want to be them?"

"Lots of people, probably."

"Aw, come on, Wylene. Are you kidding me?"

"Well, think about it," she said. "They got the only double-wide in Paradise. Their mamma looks like a fashion model just stepped off the cover of a magazine, bringing all them boyfriends home every night like life is just a party."

"You want to be her?"

Wylene shrugged. "Maybe."

Martin shook his head. He was sure he was never going to figure Wylene out. "Okay, I reckon there is somebody I'd like to be," he said.

Wylene stared at him with wide eyes. "Who?" she asked.

Martin grinned. "Ludwig van Beethoven, that's who."

Wylene laughed. "Well, the *Moonlight* Sonata sure would sound funny on a harmonica. You got to get you a real instrument if you're ever going to be Beethoven. When are you going to ask your parents about that piano I told you about? The one that girl at the plant is selling?"

"Aw, Daddy'd have a hissy fit if I even mentioned wanting a piano again," Martin said. "Besides, we don't have room for one. We don't have a double-wide like the Owenses, remember?" He smiled at Wylene, but she didn't smile back.

"You could make room if you really wanted to. You got a real knack for music, Martin. You're just wasting your God-given talents if you don't get yourself something besides a little ole harmonica to play."

She made it sound so easy. But he knew all he had to do was say the word "piano" to his father and all hell would break loose. It just wasn't worth it.

"Why don't you just go look at it," Wylene said. "It don't hurt to look."

"Naw. No use pining for something you can't never have."

"Lucky for us Mr. Beethoven didn't have your attitude, or we'd have a lot less pretty music in this world."

When the music stopped, the two of them sat in silence. Somewhere in the distance a dog barked. A baby cried. A car door slammed.

"I better go," Martin said. "See ya."

It was much cooler outside than it had been inside the trailer. Martin hadn't realized how late it had gotten. The bluish glow of television sets shone through open trailer doors. Martin took his harmonica out of his pocket and tried to play the *Moonlight* Sonata as he headed for home.

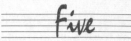

Five

SIX MILE WAS the kind of town you were born and raised in, not one you moved to from somewhere else. It wasn't surprising, then, that Martin had been the New Kid for nearly a year. Now someone else held that title.

Sybil Richards was the tallest girl Martin had ever seen. She had walked into class that morning and stared back at the sea of curious faces with a look of pure confidence. She stood up straight, not hunched over like most of the tall girls Martin knew. Her hair was cut in a perfect square around her wide face. She wore a denim skirt that nearly reached her ankles and a T-shirt that said DAYTONA INTER-NATIONAL SPEEDWAY. Silver bracelets clinked and jangled on each arm, and her big hands clutched a smudged patent leather purse.

When she walked down the aisle to an empty desk, her sandals scuffed and flapped. Some of the kids poked and jabbed one another with delight, theatrically struggling to keep from laughing. One girl laughed right out loud, a sputtering kind of laugh that shot out from between closed lips. She clamped her hand over her mouth in pretend embarrassment.

Sybil Richards sat down with a swoosh of her skirt, her bracelets clanging loudly against the desktop. She gazed back at each staring face, sending heads whipping around to face the front of the class. Martin turned quickly before her eyes had a chance to meet his.

After class, Martin hurried outside to find T.J. He spotted him with a group of kids and waited while T.J. high-fived each one before coming over to where he stood.

"Hey, Martin." T.J.'s freckled cheeks spread out in a wide grin. A baseball hat covered his buzz cut.

T.J. had an ease about him, a natural friendliness that had drawn Martin to him like a moth to a flame. He wondered how T.J. had learned to make friends so easily. Martin had moved so many times he'd never quite got the knack of it. T.J. had once begged Martin to teach him to play the harmonica. Martin had tried and tried, but T.J. just couldn't seem to get the hang of it. Maybe it was the same way with making friends. Maybe you just had to have a natural talent.

The two of them fell into step together as they headed for home. They took turns kicking a dented, rusty beer can up the side of the road.

"I guess you ain't the new kid anymore," T.J. said. He gave the can a whack with the side of his sneaker and sent it tumbling noisily along the asphalt.

"Yeah, I guess not," Martin said. He felt a wave of gratitude to Sybil Richards.

Martin ran ahead to kick the can before it rolled into a gully by the roadside. "You ever want to be somebody else, T.J.?"

"Sure, lots of times."

Martin stared at his friend. "Like who?" he said.

"Oh, I don't know. Roger Clemens or Michael Jordan or somebody like that. Or maybe that kid whose dad owns the lumberyard. He's got a van with a TV and a refrigerator in it." T.J. kept the can moving up the roadside. "How about you?"

Martin wondered if T.J. would laugh if he said Beethoven. "Naw, I can't think of anybody." He gave the can one final kick and followed T.J. into the trailer park. Now that the weather was getting warmer, doors and windows were open, spilling out the sounds of life from inside. Wylene's music drifted out through her open front door. Tammy Wynette singing, "Stand by Your Man." The words faded as the two boys continued down the road. Next came the sound of laughter from a TV, the clatter of pots and pans, the high-pitched squabbling of children. At the Owenses' trailer, T.J. pushed open the gate. A moon-shaped crevice was etched into the red dirt where the gate dragged on the ground. A BEWARE OF DOG sign hung on the chain link fence, even though the Owenses didn't have a dog. Never did have one as far as Martin knew.

"See ya," T.J. called over his shoulder before going inside.

"See ya." Martin continued down the dusty road. He lifted his chin and sang loud and off-key: "S-u-m-m-e-r-t-i-m-e, and the livin' is e-a-s-y." A dog barked at him from a neighbor's porch.

As soon as he rounded the corner, Martin saw the Furniture City delivery truck parked in front of the trailer. He stopped singing and hesitated before opening the screen door. Inside, Martin's father was watching television and sorting through a tackle box.

"Hi, Dad." Martin tossed his books onto the kitchen counter.

"Hey."

"Where's Mamma?"

Just then his mother came out from the bedroom. Her eyes were red and puffy.

"Hi, hon," she said. "I made Rice Krispie treats." She pushed a plate toward Martin. "How was school?"

"Fine." Martin took one of the sticky squares and sat on the couch. Mr. Pittman rummaged through the tackle box, untangling fishing line and picking out squiggly rubber worms.

"You going fishing, Dad?" Martin took another Rice

Krispie treat and watched his father gathering everything up and putting it back in the box.

"Thought I might," his father said. "Will you put some ice in the cooler, Doris?"

Martin's mother jerked the freezer door open and scooped ice into a cooler. Her clenched jaw pulsed slightly. An ice cube shot across the tiny kitchen and crashed to the floor, splintering into pieces, but she didn't seem to notice.

"What should I say if they call from the store?" she asked.

"Tell 'em I went fishing." Mr. Pittman winked at Martin. Martin smiled. His mother's eyes burned into him, and he looked down at the shiny little puddles of ice melting on the yellowing linoleum.

"I'm serious, Ed," Mrs. Pittman said. "You know they're gonna call."

"I don't really give a damn, Doris. I'm going fishing with my boy here." With that, he picked up his tackle box and went out. Martin followed him, waiting on the steps while his father took a six-pack of beer from the back of the furniture truck and put it in the cooler.

"You coming or not?" he called to Martin. He loaded everything into the trunk of the car and climbed in.

The car started with a roar, and a puff of black smoke shot out of the exhaust pipe. Martin hopped into the passenger side just as the car was pulling away from the trailer. The Scogginses' scruffy little dog yipped and snapped at the tires as they drove by.

Martin leaned toward the open window and let the warm air blow his hair back. They turned onto a dirt road that zigzagged through the woods. The car squeaked as it bounced along the rutted road. Every now and then the tailpipe scraped the ground. Mr. Pittman stopped the car at the edge of the lake and turned the engine off. They sat there gazing out at the glittering, still water.

"Let's go catch us some bass," his father finally said. The squeak of the car door opening broke the silence and echoed across the lake. Martin carried the fishing poles and tackle box down to the narrow beach.

"Should've got us some night crawlers," Mr. Pittman said, casting his line out into the water. "Them bass can't resist a big, juicy night crawler." He sat down with a grunt. Martin cast his line and sat down next to him.

"You ever go fishing with your daddy?" Martin asked, watching the bobber floating lazily in the still water.

His father snorted. Martin thought he wasn't going to answer, but finally he said, "Naw." They both stared out at the water in silence. Martin was thinking about how to mention the piano when his father said, "He was too busy."

"Working?"

"Chasin' skirts." Mr. Pittman's line jerked. He jumped up and reeled it in. A bass about a foot long wriggled frantically in the air. "Gotcha!" he said as he unhooked the flopping fish and tossed it into a bucket.

"Didn't Hazeline get mad?" Martin asked while his father cast his line again.

"Mad? Hell, she damn near killed him 'bout every other night. County sheriff was a regular visitor at our house."

"Were you mad when he left?" Martin said. "Your daddy,

I mean." He kept his eyes on the water. The question had just popped out, and now he wished he could take it back.

"If I'da known he was leaving, I'd have given that bastard a going-away party."

"You ever try to get in touch with him?" Martin asked.

"Nope. Never will neither."

"Seems kind of sad, not knowing where your own dad is and all." Martin watched a dragonfly hover over the water, then dart away.

His father took a swig of beer and looked at Martin. "Sad?" He chuckled and took another drink. "Son, you better toughen yourself up or you're gonna get your butt kicked out there in the real world. Sometimes fate deals out some lousy hands in life. The way I figure it, the difference between being down in the dirt miserable and full-tilt boogie on top of it all is just the luck of the draw." He took another beer out of the cooler and popped the top. "I just got me a lousy hand," he said, taking a long, gulping drink.

He nudged Martin with the cold can. "Want some?"

"Sure." Martin took a swig, then wrinkled his nose as the bitter taste filled his mouth. His eyes watered when the fizzy cold burned his throat. His father laughed. "I can see I got my work cut out for me, trying to make a man out of you."

Martin grinned sheepishly at his father. The rest of the afternoon passed in silence except for an occasional whoop when a fish bit. Just as the sun was beginning to set on the lake, turning the water a bright, iridescent pink, the sound of a motorcycle came from the road above them. It got louder and louder until the motorcycle finally burst into view with a roar, sending dust and gravel flying in all directions.

"Damn," Mr. Pittman said. "There goes another good fishing spot." He stood up and began packing up the fishing equipment.

Two people wearing helmets sat on the motorcycle looking down at Martin and his father. The driver was a man with skinny, muscular arms. His passenger was a girl, long legs sticking out of cutoff jeans.

The man turned the engine off and walked down the hill toward them. He took his helmet off and grinned.

"Hi there," he said. "How's the fishing?" He wore cowboy boots and greasy jeans. On the pocket of his blue uniform shirt was a patch that said FRANK. His face was creased and weathered. His smile exposed a row of perfect white teeth under a bushy gray mustache.

"Lousy," Martin's father said. He slammed the lid on the cooler and headed for the car.

The man's eyes darted to the bucket filled to the brim with shiny silver fish. His smile twitched a little at the corners.

"That's too bad," he said. "Reckon we'll have to find us another spot. Maybe we'll walk around to the other side. Can you get over there from here?"

"I wouldn't know." Mr. Pittman loaded the fishing gear into the trunk.

"Let's take a walk, Peanut," the man called up to the girl.

He turned and started off down the path that ran alongside the lake. A long, thin ponytail hung halfway down his back.

The girl climbed slowly off the bike. She took her helmet off and shook her square-cut hair out of her face. The cool, calm eyes of Sybil Richards gazed down at Martin. He flashed a quick, nervous smile, but she stared at him without a flicker of recognition.

"Hey, Dad," she called after the man. "Should I bring the poles?"

"Sure," he answered. "Why not?"

Sybil got the fishing poles and walked past Martin toward the lake. As she went by, she looked down at the bucket of fish and said, "I just figured we might not want to waste our time at such a lousy fishing hole, is all."

Martin watched in stunned silence as Sybil and the smiling, ponytailed man disappeared into the woods.

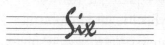

Six

"HOW'D THEM FISH taste?"

Martin looked up. Sybil Richards stood beside his chair. Without waiting for his reply, she plunked her lunch tray down on the table and sat next to him. She opened her milk carton, took a swig, then patted at the milk mustache with a napkin before picking up a greasy grilled cheese sandwich.

"Haven't had 'em yet," Martin said. "They're in the freezer."

She threw the soggy sandwich down on her plate in disgust. Her bracelets jingled as she stirred her applesauce with a fork. "I don't eat fish." She slurped the applesauce off the fork. "I'm a lacto-ovo-vegetarian."

There was no way he was going to ask what that was.

"That means I only eat vegetables, eggs, nuts, beans, and milk products," she said. "And grains. No meat, chicken, or fish. Nothing with a face, as they say."

Martin looked at his cold hamburger. This girl beat all, coming over here like the Queen of Sheba trying to ruin a perfectly good lunch.

"I just moved in with my dad," she informed him.

Martin raised his eyebrows, then took a bite of hamburger and chewed slowly, like it was the best-tasting thing he'd ever eaten.

"My brothers went to Dallas with my mom," Sybil went on. "But I said, no way, José. Not me. Nothing in Dallas but cowboys and cows." She kept stirring her applesauce and jingling her bracelets. "How come you moved to Six Mile?" she asked.

Martin held up a finger. "Excuse me," he said, "I got a mouthful of cow face." He chewed, then swallowed, ducking his head in a big, gulping motion. "Now, what was that?"

"I said how come you moved to Six Mile?"

"How do you know I moved here? Maybe I been here all my life."

"Maybe," she said, licking the back of her fork. "And maybe not." The edges of her mouth turned up into a little Mona Lisa smile. "My dad rents a house on Shaw Creek Road. I'm planting me a garden with corn and lima beans and all."

The bell rang, sending kids scrambling to clear their

places and get back to class. Martin carried his tray to the trash can and threw away the rest of his hamburger. He glanced back at Sybil. She sat there eating chocolate pudding with a fork. She smiled and wiggled her long fingers at him. "See you," she called.

Martin dropped his spoon with a clang. He kicked it out of the way and hurried out the door.

That afternoon, when Hazeline came in the front door and saw Martin's father lying on the couch, she said, "Uh-oh." She looked at Martin's mother standing at the stove, then at Martin sitting on a barstool spinning a bottle cap on the kitchen counter.

"Angela Biggins, come on down!" the announcer on TV said. Angela Biggins squealed and waved her arms as she ran down the aisle to play *The Price Is Right.*

"Somebody want to tell me what's going on?" Hazeline said, still standing in the doorway.

Angela Biggins giggled breathlessly and leaned in to the microphone. "I'm a computer programmer from Racine, Wisconsin, and the mother of two wonderful little boys, Mike and Jeffrey," she said.

Hazeline threw her bags on a chair and jammed her fists into her waist. "Okay, then, let me guess. Ed got fired."

Martin spun the bottle cap. It wobbled off the counter and onto the floor. His mother turned on the water at the sink and clattered dishes.

"Well now, ain't this a pitiful sight," Hazeline said. "Me

up here saying 'Ed got fired' like I've said about a hundred times before, and you all just sitting there like a bunch of nothing."

Martin's father sat up slowly and looked at Hazeline.

"This ain't none of your business, Mamma," he said.

"You're right, Ed. It ain't my business. But it sure as hell is theirs." She threw a bony arm in the direction of Martin and his mother. She reached into a bag for a pack of cigarettes and thumped the pack against her hand to shake one out. With quick, jerky movements, she lit it and blew out a trail of smoke, her chin pointed up in the air.

"Well, that's good, then," she said. "Now Doris can get that job she wanted over at the school, and you can stay home and cook pot roast."

"What job is that, Doris?" Mr. Pittman said. He turned off the television just as Angela Biggins was saying, "Forty-nine ninety-five?" Martin's mother stayed at the sink, her back to the room. "Just typing and answering the phone in the office," she said. "I'd be here when Martin got home." She turned around to face her husband. "I was thinking maybe I could save up for that piano Martin was wanting."

"Aw, hell, Doris, you gonna start on that again?" He looked back at the TV. "Next thing you know, he'll be wantin' a dollhouse. You gonna buy him that, too?"

Martin wished he could blink his eyes like that genie on TV and disappear in a puff of smoke.

Hazeline cleared her throat loudly. "I don't know what ya'll arguing about," she said. "Don't nobody need to work anyway. Martin's probably got twenty or thirty bottles to tide ya'll over for a few months. Ain't that right, Martin?"

Martin's chin quivered and he blinked his eyes to keep the tears from coming. Why was she making everyone look at him when he was trying so hard to disappear? He stared at the bottle cap on the floor. Then he felt Hazeline's hand on his shoulder, smelled stale cigarettes on her clothes.

"I'm sorry, hon," she said. She walked over and stood in front of her son. "You know, Ed, I been working every day of my life since I was twelve years old. I got no pity for a grown man who chooses not to support his family 'cause he ain't in the mood."

"Like my daddy supported his family, you mean?" Mr. Pittman said.

"Like I supported my family." Hazeline was yelling now. Ashes flew off the end of her cigarette as she waved her arms around. "Listen here, Ed Pittman. You been pissed off all your damn life about something can't nobody do nothing about. If you think I'm gonna get out the cryin' towel for you, you'd better think again."

She turned to Martin and said, "Why don't you get out that harmonica of yours and play 'Poor, Poor, Pitiful Me' for your daddy?"

Martin heard a laugh, and it took him a minute to realize it had come from him. Then he did something he never expected to do. He hopped off the stool and walked out the door, up the road, and down the brick path to Wylene's. He was sitting on her couch drinking a soda and watching her paint her fingernails before he realized for sure what he'd done.

"And then this guy from third shift come busting in waving a hammer like a crazy person," Wylene was saying, "And Ronnie Taylor from security tackles him right there in the weaving room, and before you know it, there's cops everywhere." She blew on her frosty pink fingernails. "Not exactly your typical day at the plant." She leaned forward and squinted at Martin. "You okay?"

"I been thinking about that piano," he said. "I was thinking maybe I could get a job and save up for it."

Wylene sat back in her La-Z-Boy reclining chair and propped her feet up. She held her hands up with her fingers spread apart like a mime touching an invisible wall. "That's great," she said.

She waved her hands around in the air to let the nail polish dry. "I'm going to put on some music to inspire you."

She picked through the tapes with stiff fingers, carefully taking one out and putting it on. "This here's Scott Joplin," she said. "This is called ragtime music. How do you like it?"

Martin grinned and slapped his leg in time to the lively music. "It's nice."

Wylene went back to the La-Z-Boy. "I bet with a little practice you could play better than that," she said. "Wouldn't it be great to just sit down and play any ole thing you felt like any ole time you wanted?" She bounced her fuzzy slippers back and forth to the music. "You could do it, Martin. I know you could. You're a natural musician."

"You think so?" Martin asked. "You really think so?"

"Sure I do. Shoot, if I had half your talent I wouldn't be wasting my time sitting around listening to somebody else. I'd be playing my heart out every minute of the day."

"You ever know any other boys that like music? I mean, you know, Beethoven and stuff like that?"

Wylene cocked her head and looked at him. "Music ain't about being a boy or being a girl, Martin. Music's about what's in your heart. If you're asking me if I've ever known anyone with as much music in their heart as you, then I reckon I'd have to say no. I ain't been that lucky."

Martin ran his fingers up and down the invisible keyboard on the coffee table, shaking his head and tapping his toes and wondering where to go from here.

Seven

MARTIN CROSSED THE highway and walked down the crumbling sidewalk, past ramshackle houses with red dirt yards. When he got to the corner, he checked out the street sign. Shaw Creek Road. Maybe he'd just take a quick walk down there before he went on home. No harm in looking, was there?

Some kids were playing kickball in the street. Martin searched their faces. His shoulders relaxed. No one he knew. He smiled at the kids, but they didn't notice.

He passed a brick ranch-style house as a woman came out of the front door. Martin walked faster, his face turned toward the street. The woman got in a car and drove away.

Martin blew out a long breath and continued down the sidewalk, peering at each house he passed.

Then he saw her. There was no mistaking that tall, standing-up-so-straight figure out in the middle of a vegetable garden. Just standing there, still as a scarecrow. What was she doing?

As Martin got closer, he realized she wasn't doing anything. Just standing there looking around at the perfectly straight rows of perfectly spaced clumps of green.

In the same instant that it occurred to Martin that he had better turn around quick and go home, Sybil Richards waved a hand over her head and called out, "Hey, Martin!"

Martin looked up in pretend surprise. Squinted at Sybil in pretend ignorance. Said, "Oh, hey," in pretend recognition. All the while still walking, getting out of there while the getting was good.

But Sybil was running after him with long, slow, loping strides. She wore the same cutoffs she had worn that day at the lake. A baseball hat was pulled down low over her eyes. Dallas Cowboys.

"Come see my garden," she said. Not "What are you doing here?" or "What a coincidence."

She tugged on Martin's arm and led him to the garden.

"The zucchini's my favorite," she said. "I love the flowers." She touched a big yellow flower gently with the toe of her sneaker.

"And okra. You ever seen an okra plant?" She pulled him to another row and picked a tiny okra off the plant. "Taste this." She took a bite and handed the rest to him. "It's better pickled. You like pickled okra?"

Martin slipped it into his pocket. No way was he eating raw okra. "Yeah, I do," he said. "But not store-bought. I only like homemade."

"Me too!" she said, high and squeaky, like it was some kind of miracle that they both preferred homemade pickled okra.

"Look at this." She pulled his arm again. Her long fingers reached all the way around his skinny wrist. He tried not to blush, but he knew that the harder he tried, the more he blushed.

They left the garden and went around behind the house. A rotting porch hung off the back of the house in midair. The wooden steps that had once gone up to it lay in a broken heap. Sybil led Martin past the porch to the back of the house and threw her arm out dramatically.

"Ta dah!" She grinned at Martin and waited for his reaction.

Martin whistled and shook his head. The entire back of the house was covered with license plates—red, green, yellow, like a giant patchwork quilt. Some of them were nothing but rust. Some were as bright and shiny as new.

"That's my favorite." Sybil pointed to South Dakota. "That's Mount Rushmore. A man named Gutzon Borglum made them faces in the rocks with drills and dynamite. Me and my dad are going there someday."

Martin studied each license plate. The Keystone State.

The Aloha State. The Peace Garden State. There were birds and flags and even the Wright Brothers' airplane.

"We've got every state except New Mexico, Land of Enchantment, and Alaska, the Last Frontier," Sybil said.

"Where'd you get all them?" Martin asked.

"Oh, all kinds of places. Flea markets, junkyards. We even found one under the porch of this very house. The Lone Star State. That's kind of an irony, don't you think?"

Martin stared blankly at her.

"My mom being in Dallas and all?" Sybil said with a touch of irritation. Like he should have remembered that her mom was in Texas.

"My dad used to drive a truck, so he's been all over," she said. "I bet he's been in nearly every one of those states. Now he's a mechanic at the Exxon station out on Walhalla Highway."

Just then a motorcycle roared up the street and into the driveway.

"Speak of the devil," Sybil said. She headed around to the front of the house, then stopped and motioned impatiently for Martin to follow.

Sybil's dad took his helmet off. He wore the same greasy jeans, same uniform shirt, same ponytail.

"Hey, Peanut," he said as Sybil gave him a peck on the cheek. He smiled and held out a greasy hand to Martin. "I'm Frank," he said.

Martin shook his hand. It was warm and rough. "I'm Martin."

"I was just showing Martin your collection," Sybil said.

"How about them?" Frank smiled at Martin, a big, eye-twinkling smile that made his mustache curl up at the ends. "You know anybody in New Mexico or Alaska?"

"No, sir, I don't." Martin wished he did.

"Oh, well. It don't hurt to ask," he said, unstrapping a grocery bag from the back of the motorcycle. "I'm going to make us some enchiladas tonight, Peanut." He tapped the bill of Sybil's hat, knocking it down over her eyes. "You want to have some enchiladas with us, Martin?"

"I better be getting home," Martin said.

"You live near here?"

"No, sir. Well, yes, kind of. I mean, near enough. See you later," he said, and walked quickly away from the little house with the rotting porch and the license plate wall. At the corner, he glanced back. Sybil and Frank stood hand in hand in the middle of the okra.

Eight

WHEN MARTIN WOKE to the sound of rain clattering on the trailer roof, he let out a contented "Aaah." What could be better than a rainy Saturday? No school and no baseball game.

He got his jeans on and headed for the kitchen, where his mother was already gathering dirty laundry.

"Seems a shame to ruin a perfectly good Saturday at the Laundromat," Martin said, stirring the pot of grits warming on the stove.

"Perfectly good? It's raining cats and dogs out there." She looked under the couch and pulled out a dusty sock. "Besides, who says I'm ruining it? The Queen Clean's my little heaven on earth. I got nothing to do there but sit. Sometimes I wish my whole life would get stuck on the spin cycle for a few weeks." She looked out the window at the rain. "Guess the good Lord answered your prayers."

Martin grinned and wiggled his eyebrows up and down. "Guess so." The rain was coming down harder now, clanging noisily on the metal roof. His father's muffled snores drifted out of the back room. "I think I'll go into town for a while, okay?"

"In this rain?"

"A little rain don't bother me."

"I can give you a ride." She tried to flatten his hair with a licked finger. "You need a haircut. And give me them jeans. They look like something the cat drug in."

"That's okay." Martin stepped out of his jeans. "I'm gonna look for bottles." He had discovered that looking for bottles was an acceptable excuse for walking.

His mother stuffed the last of the laundry into a pillowcase. "If the rain stops, I might see if I can find some flowerpots at the flea market," she said, blowing a kiss in his direction as she headed out the door.

Martin ate grits right out of the pot, then tapped a beat on the stove with the back of the spoon. His father's snores stopped, and Martin held his breath for a minute, listening. When the snoring started again, he let his breath out with a low whistle. He hurried to get dressed and grabbed one more spoonful of grits on his way out.

The unpaved road that ran through Paradise had turned

into a murky lake. Martin carried his sneakers and waded through the puddles. Gooey red mud squished up between his toes.

Within minutes, his clothes were soaked through and his hair was plastered to his head. He stopped to put his sneakers on at the WELCOME TO PARADISE sign, then started off along the side of the highway toward Pickens. There wasn't likely to be much going on in Six Mile, even on a Saturday. About the only thing that gave Six Mile the right to call itself a town was a bunch of mailboxes and a combination gas station and convenience store. The few businesses that were there were mostly in people's homes. Bernice's Beauty Spot in Bernice's kitchen. Buddy's Lawn Mower Repair in Buddy's garage.

But what Six Mile lacked in stores it made up for in churches. Freedom Baptist Church. Calvary Baptist Church. Mountainview Lutheran Church. Every week the messages on their signs changed and Martin liked to read them as he walked. "Jesus saves." "Bingo tonight." "Depart from evil, and do good; and dwell for evermore . . . Psalm 37, Verse 27."

Martin sang church songs as he walked along the muddy roadside. "Onward, Christian Soldiers." "Bringing In the Sheaves." Sometimes he and Hazeline sang church songs all the way to Howard Johnson's. Funny how folks who never stepped so much as a big toe into a church knew all the words to those songs.

Before long he was marching in time to the tunes. Right,

left, right, left. He sang louder and louder until he was almost yelling, his skinny neck stretched up like a turtle in the sun.

"Then sings my so-o-o-ul, my Savior God to thee.
How great thou a-a-art. How great thou art."

By the time Martin reached Pickens the rain had slowed to a steady drizzle. He hummed "Amazing Grace" and strolled lazily down the sidewalk. He knew the exact order of the stores. The Army Navy Store. Jimmy's Barbershop. The Blue Ridge Thrift Shop. He liked to look in the windows, but he almost never went in. Once he had bought Wylene the soundtrack from *West Side Story* at Walgreen's. But mostly he just looked.

During the week, bored store owners sat in lawn chairs on the sidewalk, watching an occasional car go by or chatting with a neighbor from the store next door. But on Saturdays, the street came alive. Mothers dragged complaining children to shop for clothes. Men got haircuts. On this particular Saturday, the rain made things seem more hurried than usual as people darted from their cars to the shelter of the stores.

Martin was weaving his way through the crowd that was beginning to form in front of the only movie theater in town when he heard his name called. He turned, searching the clusters of people huddled under umbrellas, finally spotting T.J.'s Atlanta Braves hat.

"Hey," T.J. called again as he jogged toward Martin. "You going to the movie?"

"Naw, just walking."

"The movie don't start for a few minutes yet," T.J. said. "Wanna get a Coke at Arlene's?"

"Sure." Martin pulled at his T-shirt, and it made a sucking sound.

The two boys strolled down the sidewalk, separating now and then to let people walk between them. Suddenly Martin stopped dead in his tracks.

"What's the matter?" T.J. asked.

Martin stared across the street. T.J. followed his gaze, but looked back at Martin, puzzled.

"What?" he asked.

Martin ran across the street to the window of J. H. Lawrence and Son Pawnshop. He pressed his face against the glass, cupping his hands around his eyes, and stared at the violin. It was propped up on a dented television, surrounded by dusty cases of watches and diamond rings. Its dark, rich wood was polished so shiny it practically glittered. Martin had never seen a real violin up close before. His stomach flipflopped. He felt goose bumps on his arms.

T.J.'s voice broke the spell. "What you looking at?" He stuck his face in front of Martin's to get his attention, blocking Martin's view of the window.

Martin pushed T.J. aside.

T.J. looked at the window. His eyes darted around, searching for whatever it was that Martin was looking at.

"What?" T.J. asked. "That ole fiddle?"

"Violin," Martin corrected him.

"What's the difference?" T.J. said. "You know how to play that?"

"I bet I could." Martin's fingers ached with longing to touch the violin's smooth curves. He ran his finger along the window glass, following the strings up the slender neck and tracing the curly scroll at the end.

"I'm going in," Martin said, starting for the door.

"What for?"

"I want to look at that violin."

"How come?"

"Just curious is all."

T.J. lifted his shoulders and let them drop again. "I'm going on back to the movie, then," he said.

Martin wiped his hands on his jeans. A bell tinkled when he opened the pawnshop door. His wet sneakers made a squishy sound when he walked. The shop was dark and damp and smelled like mothballs. Every available space had been put to use. Rifles and moth-eaten deer heads hung on the wall. Stereos were stacked in corners. A smudged glass display case was filled with wedding rings, pocket watches, and cameras.

Martin called, "Hello?" His voice sounded eerie in the quiet shop. He waited a minute before calling again. "Anybody here?"

Finally a man pushed aside a curtain and came out of a back room, carrying a steaming mug of coffee.

"Yes?" he said, eyeing Martin suspiciously.

"You Mr. Lawrence?"

The man nodded. Martin jerked his head toward the window. "How much is that violin?"

Mr. Lawrence went over and peered at the violin in the window, as if he had a whole roomful of violins and needed to know exactly which violin Martin was talking about.

He took a sip of coffee, squinting his eyes in the steam and making a slurping noise. "Fifty," he said.

"I'd like to see it, please," Martin said. He straightened his shoulders, trying to look mature, and brushed the wet hair off his forehead.

Mr. Lawrence eyed him. "You got fifty bucks?" he asked.

"Was that fifty to see or fifty to buy?"

Mr. Lawrence's expression changed. His eyebrows shot up into two arches of disapproval. He started to say something, then put the coffee mug down so hard coffee sloshed over the sides. He stepped over boxes, stereo speakers, and car radios till he could reach into the window for the violin. Martin tried to keep his hands from shaking as he reached for it. He hesitated, not sure how to hold it. Somehow it seemed rude to hold the violin in the wrong place— like dancing with a girl, afraid to put your hand too low on her back or too high on her side. Mr. Lawrence was getting impatient, so Martin just reached for the neck. The violin was surprisingly light. Martin ran his hand along the curves. He stroked the smooth back, then carefully turned it over and ran a finger along the strings.

He looked up at Mr. Lawrence. "Is there a bow that goes with it?" He grinned, trying to look like this was about the four hundredth violin he'd held in his lifetime. No big deal. Just another ole violin.

"Yeah, there's a bow that goes with it. When it's sold. You buying it?"

"Maybe."

"Look, kid, I ain't got all day. You want it or not?"

"Would you take thirty dollars for it?" Martin couldn't believe he had said that. First of all, he'd never bargained with anybody in his life. And second of all, he didn't have thirty dollars.

Mr. Lawrence's answer was short and to the point. "Nope."

Martin kept stroking the strings, stalling for time while he tried to figure out what to do next.

Mr. Lawrence reached for the violin. "This violin's only been here a month. I've already lowered the price more than I ought to. Either you want it or you don't."

He took the violin from Martin and put it back in the window, then went back to his coffee as if Martin had just disappeared.

Martin turned in his squishy sneakers and left. The rain had stopped and the street was already beginning to dry. Steam drifted up from the hot pavement. Martin watched his feet as he walked, chanting softly to the steady rhythm. Left, right, left, right. How else was he going to keep all those violin thoughts from flailing around in his head like a cat in a bag?

He took a detour from his usual route and turned down Shaw Creek Road. Sybil's house was quiet. Frank's motorcycle was parked in the driveway. Martin walked by slowly, trying to see through the screen door into the darkness inside. What were they doing in there? Martin imagined the two of them sitting at the kitchen table, drinking iced tea and eating pickled okra. Sharing jokes. Laughing. Planning their trip to South Dakota.

When he got home, Martin went straight to his bedroom. He closed the door and stretched out on his bed, looking up at the water-stained ceiling. He sniffed his fingers. The smell of the oily wood of the violin lingered on his fingertips. He reached under his bed and pulled out a battered shoe box, dumping the contents on the bed. Three arrowheads. A picture of a dog he used to have. A bird's nest. A real Japanese fan Hazeline had won playing bingo. A small leather pouch. He opened the pouch and counted the money inside. Twelve dollars and seventy-eight cents. A long way from fifty dollars.

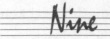

Nine

"Earth to Martin. Earth to Martin." The entire American history class exploded in laughter. Martin jumped and sat up straight.

"Yes, sir?" he said, keeping his eyes on his desk. He traced the carving in the grimy wood with his finger. Jo Ellen Loves Roy.

"You care to join us, Mr. Pittman?" the teacher said.

Martin said, "Yes, sir," although actually no, he didn't care to join them. He'd rather have stayed where he'd been before he was so rudely interrupted. Playing the violin. Outdoors somewhere. Nobody else around. Nobody scuffing their shoes or thumping their pencils or popping their chewing gum.

Martin watched the minute hand on the clock over the door jerk straight up. He was out the door and halfway down the hall before the bell had finished ringing. He turned toward the main office, ducking and dodging the rush of kids scurrying in the opposite direction. Outside the guidance counselor's office, Martin stopped to examine the bulletin board that covered the dirty wall. It was a crazy quilt of notices and fliers. Charlene needed a ride to Atlanta. Randy would paint, do yard work, or house-sit. Candace W. was looking for a nonsmoking baby-sitter for three small children.

"You want free rabbits?"

Martin turned to see Sybil inspecting the bulletin board, her hands jammed into the pockets of her baggy jeans. One toe of her sneakers was covered with silver duct tape.

Martin ran his hand over the top of his head. "Nope," he said. "I used to have a rabbit."

Sybil cocked her head. "What happened to it?"

"I turned it loose in the woods."

"How come?"

Martin grinned. "It was Easter."

Sybil smiled and looked back at the bulletin board. "What are you looking for?" she asked.

"Just looking."

"Need a job?"

Martin shot her a look. How come she always knew so much about him? This girl was downright spooky sometimes. "I need thirty-seven dollars and twenty-two cents," he said, pretending to read a notice on the bulletin board.

Why had he said that? What was he going to say when she asked, "What for?"

"Me, I just like to look," she said. "You never know what you might find on a bulletin board. My mom found a divorced white male looking for a fun-loving, romantic blonde. Only problem was he forgot to mention that he didn't have a job, is ugly as sin, and was going to move in with his sister in Dallas. Then again, I guess my mom didn't see that as a problem, seeing as how she hightailed it out to Dallas like a dog in heat."

Sybil slung her backpack over her shoulder. "Good luck finding a job," she said.

Her baggy jeans flapped as she walked away, making a whooshing sound that echoed in the empty hallway. Martin waited until she was out of sight before following her. Just as he opened the big double doors and went out into the bright sunlight, Sybil was skateboarding down the sidewalk, her jeans billowing out like sails on a sailboat. As she passed, she looked at Martin and saluted. He tried not to, but he couldn't stop himself. He smiled and saluted back.

Martin went back to Pickens twice to make sure the violin was still there. He hadn't gone into the shop, just stood outside staring in the window, imagining that he was playing the violin.

Once a woman had stood beside him, looking in the window, too. Martin's stomach had balled up tight, and his heart had jumped clean up into his throat. It hadn't occurred to him that anyone else had a perfect right to walk into that shop and buy his violin. He had watched the woman out of the corner of his eye. When she leaned over and squinted to get a better look at something, he followed her gaze. A gold locket in a velvet case. Martin nearly jumped up and kissed her.

He felt like he was going to bust wide open if he didn't tell somebody about the violin. For the longest time, he had been afraid that if he said the words out loud, the violin might disappear. Martin believed a broken mirror guaranteed a person seven years' bad luck. He avoided anything with the number 13 on it. Hadn't stepped on a sidewalk crack in his whole life. And up to now, he had been pretty lucky about most things. He didn't want to spoil his luck, but it seemed like the time had come to tell Wylene.

"Shoot," Martin said under his breath when he heard the music floating out of Wylene's trailer. Frank Sinatra poor-me-I'm-so-lonesome-and-nobody-loves-me songs. That meant Wylene was in a mood. Sure enough, she came to the door red-nosed and teary-eyed.

"Hey," Martin said with exaggerated cheeriness. He pretended not to notice her pouty mouth.

"Hey." She flipped up the latch on the screen door but didn't open it for him.

Inside the trailer, Martin had to adjust his eyes to the darkness. A fan whirred back and forth in the corner. It was barely four o'clock in the afternoon, but Wylene had her bathrobe on.

"Fourteen more days of school," Martin said. He stuck a

finger in the parakeet cage and let Pudgie peck it. "I sure got me a case of summer fever."

"Mmmm." Wylene propped her feet up on the coffee table and fanned herself with a *Reader's Digest*.

"What's the matter?" Martin couldn't believe he had asked that. He felt like a big ole trout being reeled into the boat.

Wylene took a deep breath and let it out in a gush of a sigh. "I don't know," she said, shaking her head slowly and looking down at her slippers. "You know, every night I go to bed telling myself tomorrow's a new day. And every morning I wake up saying today I'll be happy. But somewhere between waking up and going to bed again, Mr. Sad and Lonely sneaks in and grabs me. And no matter how hard I try, I can't shake him off."

Suddenly resentment oozed over Martin like a quart of molasses in a pint jar. Finding that violin was about the best thing that had ever happened to him. He had come here ready to share his good news with his closest friend, and there she sat in a red bathrobe crying for no good reason.

"I found a violin," he blurted out.

Wylene stopped fanning and looked at him.

"A what?"

"A violin."

They stared at each other for a minute. The fan whirred soothingly back and forth. Frankie crooned on about strangers in the night.

Wylene sat up. The sag in her shoulders lifted. "Where?"

"Pickens. In a pawnshop."

"Well, I'll be."

Funny, now that he had told her, Martin didn't know what to say next.

"Well?" Wylene said, dipping her head slightly in anticipation.

"Well . . ." Martin looked around the room. He had thought so much about that violin, but sitting here in Wylene's trailer actually talking about it made him realize that most of his thoughts had been fantasies, crazy little dreams that were about as far away from reality as an acorn from an oak tree.

"Well?" Wylene said again.

"Well, I don't know."

"What do you mean, you don't know?" Wylene looked at him like he was some kind of lunatic or something. He was beginning to wish he hadn't told her.

"I mean, I don't know," he said a little louder.

"Well, don't you see? That's the perfect instrument for you, Martin." Wylene stood up. "I don't know why I never thought of it before. It's much better than a piano! It's small. It don't take up a bit of space. You could keep it right under your bed. And you can play all kinds of music on it. It's practically the sweetest-sounding instrument there is." She paced back and forth, gesturing excitedly. "I mean, it's perfect." She drew the last word out long and loud, then stopped suddenly and looked at Martin.

"Well?" she said again.

"There's only one problem," Martin said. "I don't have fifty dollars."

"Well, get fifty dollars."

"How?"

"I don't know. Sell something. Collect bottles. Get a paper route. For heaven's sake, Martin, it ain't fifty million dollars."

"The money's not the problem."

"Then what is the problem?"

"There ain't no way Daddy's gonna let me have a violin."

There! He had said it at last, the thought that had been there since the first moment he had stood in front of J. H. Lawrence and Son. The thought that had been so tiny and hidden away, but he had known it was there. Like a chigger you can't see but sure can feel the itch of.

Wylene looked at him with one of the calmest faces he'd ever seen her wear.

"Well then," she said slowly, "you just explain to your daddy that you have a gift. That the good Lord has blessed you with the gift of music."

"I don't think he wants to hear about the good Lord, Wylene."

"Then you tell him to mind his own damn business and leave you the hell alone!"

Martin stared at Wylene, his mouth hanging open. He had never heard Wylene so much as raise her voice, and now she was doing it and using cuss words to boot.

Wylene sat down and took a deep breath. She looked at

Martin with such serious eyes he couldn't look back at her. He wove his fingers in and out of the crocheted afghan folded neatly on the back of the couch, trying to prepare himself for whatever serious thing she was about to say.

"I would never in my life hurt your feelings on purpose, Martin," she said. "You been a good friend to me. Better than anybody else. Better than my own kin even. That's why it hurts me to watch you being kicked around like a stray cat."

She leaned forward and peered into Martin's face. "I sit here every weekend and watch you go off to them ball games, and it dern near tears my heart out," she continued. "I can't help but wonder what kind of daddy would make his son do something that was so against his nature—and then add insult to injury by denying him what he was put on this earth to love."

Martin cleared his throat. He picked dirt out of his fingernails. He looked at the clock and was relieved to see it wasn't suppertime yet. He felt a long walk coming on.

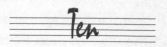

Ten

"HOT KRISPY KREMES," Hazeline sang as she came into the trailer.

"You're late." Ed Pittman didn't look up from the TV.

"Well, good morning to you, too, Sunshine," Hazeline said, a cigarette bobbing up and down in the corner of her mouth. "Mmmm, don't these smell good?"

Martin hurried over to get a doughnut. He took a bite of the warm, sweet dough. There was nothing in the world like a Krispy Kreme doughnut. It was like biting into a sugar-coated cloud. Hazeline had a knack for getting to the doughnut shop when the doughnuts were still hot.

"What time is this damn game, anyway?" she asked.

Mr. Pittman cocked his head and looked at her out of the corner of his eye. "This damn game is in twenty minutes. And if Zsa Zsa Gabor in there don't get a move on, we're gonna be late.

"Move it, Doris!" he yelled, making Martin jump.

Martin wiped his sticky fingers on his baseball uniform and took another doughnut. Usually before a game he was too nervous to eat. But today was different. Ever since he'd seen the violin, he'd felt different about everything—even baseball. He couldn't figure out exactly how or why. He just knew he did. A little more peaceful, maybe. It was almost as if the violin had given him the tiniest little glimpse into a future that could be his. At first he had wanted that violin so bad he was ready to run back to Pickens and throw a rock through the pawnshop window to get it. He'd take the next Greyhound bus to anywhere, just him and his violin. But of course that idea had simmered down to more rational thinking. That was where he was now—rational thinking. But rational thinking was an art he hadn't quite perfected yet.

"I'm coming." Doris Pittman came out of the tiny bedroom yanking pink curlers out of her hair. "I smell doughnuts."

"Why you making Martin do this, Ed?" Hazeline asked, glaring at her son, her hands on her hips, skinny elbows jutting out to the side.

"Do what, Mamma?" Mr. Pittman asked.

"This baseball crap is what."

"I don't consider baseball crap."

"Well, maybe Martin considers baseball crap. You ever think of asking him?" For such a small woman, Hazeline had a way of filling up the whole trailer.

Martin's father turned. "You consider baseball crap, son?" he asked slowly.

"No, sir."

Behind him, Hazeline snorted and snuffed her cigarette out in the sink. In this family there was no way to agree with one without disagreeing with the other.

No one spoke on the way to the game. When Hazeline went that long without talking, it was a pretty safe bet she wasn't happy. Martin's father cursed when the car hit a pothole in the road. His mother hummed softly in the front seat. Martin tapped his foot in time to the humming, trying to figure out what song it was till he realized it was just a nervous, filling-in-the-quiet kind of tune.

By the time they got to the ballpark, the game had begun. Martin wasn't even out of the car yet before he heard Riley Owens.

"Thank goodness," Riley said in a prissy voice. "Martin Armpit's here. I was so worried he wasn't gonna make it." Riley grinned at the row of girls giggling beside him. "This team would be in big trouble without Martin Armpit."

Hazeline rolled down the car window and yelled, "Shut up, Riley." Martin flushed when the girls laughed even harder.

"That punk gets my goat worse than anybody else alive," she muttered.

"For once we agree on something, Mamma," Martin's father said.

Martin helped his mother with the lawn chairs and cooler.

"Get on over there, Martin," his father said, jabbing a thumb in the direction of the bench.

Martin couldn't have been on a more perfect team. They were lousy hitters, which meant they struck out so fast he hardly ever came up to bat. And they had T.J. for a pitcher. T.J. was the best pitcher in Six Mile, maybe the best in the whole county. Thanks to him, their team's time in the outfield was usually cut so short Martin hardly even touched the ball, only occasionally heard the dreaded sound of the bat hitting the ball, signaling the possibility that he would be expected to catch.

Catching was something other kids must have been born knowing how to do. They were always throwing and catching things like it was no big deal—apples on the school bus, borrowed pencils in class, quarters in the cafeteria. But to Martin, catching seemed about as natural as socks on a rooster. When he was little, his father was all the time hollering, "Catch!" Martin would freeze as some object came hurtling toward him. A lifetime of practicing hadn't made one bit of improvement. All he could do in a ball game was cross his fingers and hope the ball didn't come his way—and thank T.J. for being such a good pitcher.

Usually when Martin stood out in right field, he felt sick. His head hurt, his stomach churned, and his mouth went dry. But today he was almost enjoying himself. The warm

May sun on his face made him drowsy. In his head he played slow, soft concertos on the violin. He wanted to lie down in the sweet-smelling clover and listen. Not even the sound of the bat hitting the ball rattled his good feeling today. When he missed a ground ball coming right to him, he didn't even care about the kids yelling at him, didn't think about what his father would say.

Once he glanced over at his family. Hazeline hooted and hollered at the umpire, shaking a skinny fist. His father paced by the bleachers, throwing his arms up and talking to the sky. Martin smiled and went back to his concertos.

When the game was over, he knew his team had lost by the sad faces and drooping shoulders of his teammates. He whistled on his way back to the car. His father slammed the trunk. "You even know what the score was?" he said.

"No, sir."

"You beat anything I ever seen, Martin."

Hazeline stuck her head out of the car window. "Get in the car, Ed."

Mr. Pittman jerked the door open and got in. Martin climbed in the back beside Hazeline.

"You can wipe that smirk off your face," his father said.

Martin looked out the window at the other boys with their families.

"We have to go through this every damn time," Hazeline said.

Martin's father hit the steering wheel. "No we don't. Maybe just one time Martin would stop picking daisies in the outfield and play the game."

"Can we go home now?" Hazeline said. "I'm getting a headache."

As they pulled out of the parking lot, Martin watched a group of boys pile into a van. He tried to picture himself climbing in with them. Cracking jokes and poking ribs. Maybe grabbing someone's baseball hat for a friendly game of keep-away. When the van disappeared from sight, Martin looked around the car at his family. The back of his father's thick, tense neck, his hands clenched on the steering wheel. His mother gazing off into the distance, the edges of her mouth lined and droopy, her eyes dreamy. Hazeline, her arms crossed tightly, an unlit cigarette dangling from the corner of her mouth. Martin caught a glimpse of himself in the rearview mirror. He was smiling. He closed his eyes, leaned his head against the back of the seat, and listened to concertos the rest of the way home.

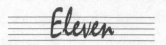

Eleven

MARTIN HAD A NUMBER of things to worry about, but the biggest worry—the one with the capital "W"—was the possibility that the violin might be sold to someone else. Some people were good at worrying. They stewed and fretted right in the middle of living a normal life. Take Wylene, for instance. She'd say, "I'm really worried that cat's gonna have her kittens under my trailer." And then she'd go on off to work just like normal. But Martin couldn't seem to fit worrying in with the rest of his life. When he worried, everything else had to wait.

School was out. Baseball was over. Summer had charged right in like a mad bull. But Martin was too worried to think about all those good things crammed into life at once. Finally he decided to put a temporary hold on worrying—and he'd figured out just how to do it.

Just the deciding it had freed up his mind enough to let a song in as he headed toward Pickens. "B-I-N-G-O," he sang, bobbing his head and swinging his arms to the beat. When the tune was over, he listened to the rhythm of summer sounds. Lawn mowers and sprinklers. Jump ropes and ice cream trucks. He waved to a lady selling peaches from the back of her pickup. Maybe on the way back he'd buy some so his mother could make a peach cobbler.

He didn't slow down when he got to Main Street. He walked past the Army Navy Store, Jimmy's Barbershop, and the Blue Ridge Thrift Shop, across the street, and right into J. H. Lawrence and Son Pawnshop. He glanced in the window on his way in, scared that if he looked a second too long, the violin wouldn't be there.

Mr. Lawrence was behind the counter eating pork and beans out of a can. Martin got right to the point.

"If I give you a deposit, could you hold that violin for a while?"

Mr. Lawrence looked at him, chewing slowly. "That's not my customary method of conducting business," he said.

"I can appreciate that, Mr. Lawrence." Martin's worry was starting to bubble up inside him again. "I can give you ten dollars." As soon as he said it, Martin realized that ten dollars didn't sound like much. It had felt like a lot more in his pocket.

Mr. Lawrence smiled. "I'm running a business here, son. This ain't no Salvation Army."

"Just hold it for two weeks. Don't let nobody else buy it and . . . and . . ." Martin paused, searching for something, anything, that would persuade Mr. Lawrence. "And you can keep the ten. I'll pay the whole fifty when I pick it up."

Mr. Lawrence wiped his mouth and made little sucking noises while he cleaned his teeth with his tongue. Finally he said, "One week. I'll hold it one week. No longer."

Martin slapped two fives into Mr. Lawrence's upturned palm. "You got yourself a deal."

Martin was halfway home before he realized his mistake. What he'd gone and done was swap one worry for another. Now he only had one week to convince his father to let him buy the violin—and then come up with fifty dollars. He might as well have been worrying about how to flap his arms and fly to the moon.

When he turned in to Paradise, he heard the thwack of a baseball hitting a glove. T.J. and Riley were throwing the ball to each other in the road.

"Hey, Martin," T.J. called without looking at him. Martin was impressed that T.J. could talk and still keep the smooth, even rhythm of throwing and catching.

"Hey," Martin said, sitting on the ground by the road to watch. He took his sneakers off and wiggled his feet around in the cool grass.

"Where you been, Armpit?" Riley asked. Throw. Thwack. Throw. Thwack.

"Pickens."

"What for?"

"Just felt like it."

Riley grinned. "You ain't two-timin' Wylene, now, are you, Pitts?" Thwack went the ball.

"Shut up, Riley." All Martin's worrying was beginning to make him irritable. "What ya'll doing this summer?" he asked, to change the subject.

"Vacation Bible school." Riley laughed so hard he missed T.J.'s pitch. "I'm going to get my smokes," he said and took off for the trailer.

After retrieving the ball, T.J. came over and sat down beside Martin. "I wish I could get me a job," he said. "Winn Dixie's hiring bag boys, but Mamma says she needs me around to watch Becky. Having a little sister sure is a pain. How about you?" he asked, tossing the baseball from hand to hand.

Martin shrugged. "I don't know. Get some lawn-mowing jobs, I reckon. Maybe I'll check out the Winn Dixie. I need to make some money this summer."

"You gonna buy that ole fiddle?" T.J. blew a bubble with his gum until it popped, covering his nose with pink film.

"Naw," Martin answered. He watched the baseball plop back and forth in T.J.'s hands. He didn't dare look up. He could feel his eye twitching, knew his face was red.

Why was he lying to T.J.? Why couldn't he just say, I sure would like to buy it, if I could?

For a minute Martin felt like he was going to cry. Felt like his feelings were just going to bust right out of him. He kept watching the ball, back and forth, back and forth, till he got control of himself and pushed his feelings back down again.

Riley sauntered over, smoking a cigarette. "What you doin' this summer?" he asked Martin. "Besides hanging around with Lard-Ass Lundsford, that is." He snatched the ball from T.J. and tossed it straight up, catching it in his baseball hat. "What you two do in there all day anyways, Pitts? Practice the tango or something?"

"We listen to music. There a law against that?"

"Hey, don't get all riled up now. I was just curious, is all. I mean, I hear ya'll in there every damn day."

"What kind of music ya'll listen to?" T.J. asked.

Martin picked at the grass, wiggled dirt out from between his toes. "All kinds," he said.

"Mostly love songs, right, Armpit?" Riley said.

"Actually, my favorite is Beethoven. Ya'll like Beethoven?" Martin grinned at Riley.

Riley poked T.J. in the ribs. "Beethoven? Ain't that a coincidence? That's T.J.'s favorite, too, ain't it, T.J.?" He hooted and lay down, covering his face with his baseball hat.

Martin stood up. "See ya'll later." He headed for his trailer. He'd had more than his daily dose of Riley Owens. Besides, he'd let himself have ten whole minutes of normal life. Now the worry was starting to creep back in.

Twelve

THIS IS GONNA be the day. This is gonna be the day. This is gonna be the day, Martin said to himself when he opened his eyes Sunday morning. He said it while he brushed his teeth. He said it as he sopped his waffle in a puddle of syrup. Today was definitely going to be his lucky day. The day he'd ask his father about the violin. The day things started going his way.

He'd lain in bed the night before and thought about the best way to do it. Should he wait till he and his father were alone? Should he talk to his mother first? Maybe it would be better to wait for Hazeline and have the whole family together. Finally he decided to follow his instincts. Martin had always had pretty good instincts. He would know when the time was right.

"Why don't you and Hazeline eat here today?" his mother said, turning a piece of chicken, golden and crisp, in the sizzling oil.

"Fine with me," Martin said, mopping the last drop of syrup off his plate with his finger. He watched his mother take the chicken out of the skillet and pour in milk. She scraped the browned, crusty chicken skin off the bottom of the pan and stirred until the gravy was thick and smooth. Martin's mouth watered. The Prince of Wales buffet was good, but nothing could beat his mother's fried chicken with cream gravy. To go with it, she'd serve all his favorites—potato salad, black-eyed peas, sliced tomatoes, green beans cooked all day with a ham hock. There was no way Mr. Howard Johnson could do better than that.

Martin heard the Studebaker pull up and went to the door.

"Guess what I got," Hazeline called as she collected her bags.

Martin knew better than to try. When he was little, he'd call out everything he could think of. A telephone, roller skates, a puppy. He had never in his whole life been right. Eventually he quit trying. At least, he'd tried to quit. Hazeline loved guessing games.

"Aw, come on," she would say. "Guess." Or, "Come on. I'll give you three guesses."

Martin held the door open for her. From the looks of it,

one of the bags held something heavy. Martin decided to test his luck and give it a shot.

"A bowling ball."

"Close." Hazeline grinned. "Guess again."

"I give up."

"A watermelon." Hazeline proudly plunked a round, green melon onto the kitchen counter. "But not just a ordinary ole watermelon."

Somehow that didn't surprise Martin.

"Anybody here ever seen a yellow watermelon?" She got a knife out of the kitchen drawer and sliced into the melon. "Look at this."

The melon fell into two pieces. Sure enough, it was golden yellow inside.

"Well, I'll be," Martin said.

His father came out of the bedroom, scratching his hairy white stomach.

"Look at this, Daddy," Martin said. "A yellow watermelon. Ain't that something?"

His father eyed the melon suspiciously. "Well," he said, "I have to admit, that is something."

"How you reckon they do that?" Martin said.

"Who knows?" Hazeline said, cutting a slice of watermelon and handing it to Martin. "Bunch of weird scientists sittin' around playing God. Too bad they don't invent something more useful, like a money tree. Wouldn't none of us have to work then."

Martin tensed when he heard the word "work." He closed

his eyes and waited for his father's angry outburst. He could hardly believe his ears when he heard his father chuckle. "And what would you do with a money tree, Mamma?" his father asked, cutting a piece of melon and eating it right off the knife.

"Depends on if it was a big money tree or a little money tree," Hazeline said, lighting a cigarette and climbing up on a barstool. "If it was just a little one, I'd get some new tires for that pile of junk called a car out there. If it was a big money tree, I'd push that thing off the nearest cliff and go to Hawaii with some cute young cowboy in skintight jeans." She laughed her wheezy laugh and winked at Martin.

They all laughed, all of them at the same time. That was a good sign. That was definitely a good sign.

"You know, I saw me a violin in Pickens the other day." Martin said it to the walls, the floor, the air. "I was thinking maybe that'd be a good instrument to have, being a good size and all. I mean, it don't take up a lot of room like a piano . . . and I could play all kinds of music on it. You know, country and western, church music, maybe even some classical if I wanted to. I never played a violin before, but I bet I could learn. I wouldn't need no lessons, though. I'm sure of that. I kind of got an ear for music. I bet anything I could learn to play it by myself, like I did the harmonica. And this here's a real good violin. But it only costs fifty bucks. I bet most violins cost twice that. I was thinking maybe you could give it to me for my birthday and then I'd pay you back some of the money. Or all the money. I could pay back all the money."

When Martin finally stopped, he couldn't remember a thing he had said. He wondered if it had come out the way he'd rehearsed it in his head. He took a bite of watermelon and concentrated on sorting out the seeds in his mouth. He watched a fly land in a puddle of melon juice on the counter. Suddenly his father did the worst thing he could have done. He laughed. Martin swallowed the melon, seeds and all.

"Well now, don't that beat all?" his father asked, looking around at everyone, smiling, shaking his head. "Martin wants a violin. Let me see if I can guess whose idea that was."

Martin stared at his father. "It was my idea," he said.

"Your idea." His father jabbed the watermelon with the knife, letting the words hang in the air. "Yours and who else's, Martin?"

Martin had been prepared for an argument about the violin, but the conversation was taking a turn he hadn't expected.

"Just mine," he said.

His father narrowed his eyes to a mean squint. Martin looked away. "Martin," his father said, "I'm gonna to tell you somethin' and I want you to listen good 'cause I'm only gonna tell you once. I will not tolerate this. You spend all your time with some damn weirdo twice your age, and now you come home and start this crap. Well, Martin, what Wylene Lundsford does in her home is her business, but when she starts turning my son into some kinda damn queer boy, then it becomes my business. And I will not tolerate it."

"Oh, for cryin' out loud, Ed," Hazeline interrupted. "I

don't know what you're getting at, but I think you're straying from the subject a bit here. The boy just wants a violin. What's so damn bad about that?"

"All right, Mamma. I'll get back to the subject. Martin ain't gettin' no violin."

Martin looked from one to the other. What could he say now? Could he, by some miracle, come up with a line that would change his father's mind? Or was he just going to let that violin slip right on out of his life without ever having uttered a word? He looked at his mother. Why didn't she say something? Why didn't she help him?

Hazeline's angry voice interrupted his thoughts. "Why you just standin' there like a bump on a log, Martin? You want that violin so bad, why don't you take up for yourself?"

Martin stared at her for a moment before dropping his eyes. He knew the answer to that question. Knew he'd put so much energy into pushing down what he wanted and who he was that he just didn't have enough energy left over to fight back.

But when he opened his mouth, the words that came out were "I don't know."

Thirteen

THE NOONDAY SUN was so hot that little bubbles of melted tar dotted the road. By the time Martin got to Sybil's, the bottoms of his bare feet were crusted with the thick, gooey stuff. He went around back to the garden. Sybil sat in a lawn chair with her head down.

"Hey," he called.

She looked up and waved a postcard in the air. "From my mom," she said.

Martin sat down in the grass beside her chair. "You miss her?"

"Not enough to go to Texas like she's trying to get me to do." Sybil turned the postcard over and over in her hand.

"Besides, I don't need to hear how my clothes are too sloppy and my hair's too stringy and my fingernails look ugly all chewed up."

"Do you think your mom likes you?" Martin asked.

Sybil shrugged. "I guess so," she said. "I never thought about it."

"I mean, do you think she'd like you better if you quit biting your fingernails or ironed your clothes or something?" Martin watched a dragonfly swooping around the backyard.

"Naw. She'd just find something else I could do better."

"Don't that bother you?"

"Nope." Sybil studied the postcard on her lap: an armadillo saying, "Wish you were here."

"How come?" Martin asked.

" 'Cause I think I'm fine just the way I am."

Martin looked at Sybil, sitting in the lawn chair like the Queen of Cool, her long legs stretched out in front of her. Something mighty admirable about a kid who could talk like that. He took his harmonica out of his shirt pocket and played "The Yellow Rose of Texas."

Sybil stood up and grinned down at him. "I never knew you could play the harmonica," she said. "Where you been hiding that?"

"I ain't been hiding it," Martin said.

Sybil sat on the grass next to him. "I wish I could play an instrument."

"Really?"

"Sure."

"Like what?"

"I don't know. Anything." She looked at the harmonica in Martin's hand. "What other instrument can you play?"

Martin pulled at a blade of grass and threw it at his feet. "I don't know. My dad won't give me a chance to find out."

"What does that mean?"

"Means he don't like nothing about me." Martin could feel Sybil looking at him, but he kept pulling the grass, throwing the grass.

Sybil lay back with her hands under her head and crossed one foot over the other. Martin put his harmonica to his mouth and played. "Amazing Grace." "Camptown Races." "Zip-A-Dee-Doo-Dah." Whatever came to mind.

Every now and then he glanced over at Sybil. There wasn't much in this world that could have made him feel good about himself right then, but her smiling face and rocking feet came close.

Every time Martin started to tell Wylene what his dad had said about the violin, he got so weighed down with bad feelings he couldn't talk. Just saying the words in his head was bad enough. Telling it out loud seemed nearly impossible. But he knew she was going to ask sooner or later, so one day he just up and told her everything that had happened on that day which was supposed to have been his lucky day. She sat in the La-Z-Boy in front of the fan, eating ice cream out of a Dixie cup. She had on her Hav-a-Hanky shirt, the armpits wet with perspiration.

When he finished, she set the cup down and looked at him with an I-told-you-so expression on her face.

"Am I supposed to be surprised?" she said.

Martin felt a flicker of anger. "No."

"Well, what are you going to do?"

"There ain't nothing I can do, Wylene. I guess fate just dealt me a lousy hand."

Wylene sat on the edge of her chair and leaned toward him. "What are you talking about, Martin? A lousy hand. That don't sound like you. Besides, this ain't no big poker game of life or something. This is your chance to do what you've always wanted to do. To be what you've always wanted to be. If fate has dealt you a hand, it's the hand of music. You are a musician, Martin. You just gonna let that slip on by like a ship passin' in the night?"

Martin wanted to leave. He wanted to lie in his bed with the covers over his head. Instead, he slouched down lower on the couch, his skinny legs stretched out in front of him, knocking the toes of his sneakers together.

"You know, Wylene," he said, running a hand over the top of his head. "It might sound crazy, but I don't think my daddy likes me. I mean, I reckon he loves me 'cause I'm his son and all. But he don't like me."

He looked down at his feet and hesitated a minute before continuing.

"But you know what the worst part is? The worst part is I don't think I like him, either."

There. He had said it. He hoped Wylene wouldn't say

anything. He waited. She didn't. He felt a surge of fondness for her because she knew him so well.

"I been doing a lot of thinking lately," he said.

"Thinkin' about what?" Wylene said softly.

"Oh, just about everything. Questions mostly." He closed his eyes when the fan swung slowly in his direction and blew cool air in his face.

"You know what I'm beginning to think?" he said. "I'm beginning to think maybe the answer to most questions is 'just because.' You know what I mean?"

Wylene nodded, not like she was saying yes but like she was pondering what he was saying.

"Why's my daddy so angry all the time? Just because. Why don't he like it that I'd rather have a violin than a baseball bat? Just because. Why don't my mamma just bust him in the chops and get the hell outa Dodge? Just because. See what I mean?"

Wylene pushed her damp, frizzy hair up off the back of her neck when the fan whirred in her direction. "I think there's another question you should add to that list," she said.

Martin arched his eyebrows and waited.

"Why do you keep trying to please somebody you don't even like?" she said.

"Aw, hell, Wylene . . ." Martin punched the throw pillow beside him.

"I mean, pardon my ignorance, Martin, but I just don't understand why . . ."

"That's just it, Wylene." Martin pulled his feet in and sat up straight. "You don't understand. Nobody does." He dropped against the back of the couch again. "I don't even know if I do."

They sat there for a minute, both of them staring at something but not seeing it. Then Martin sat up and took his harmonica out of his pocket. He cupped his hands around it and played slow and soft. Wylene pushed the La-Z-Boy back to a reclining position, folded her hands on her stomach, and listened. After a while Martin changed to a fast, lively tune. He rocked his body back and forth and tapped his toe on the floor. Wylene nodded her head and clapped her hands, a little smile on her face.

"You know," she said when he finished, "Beethoven believed that music could change the world. I don't know about that, but it sure can change a mood, can't it?"

Martin said yes, but he was lying. His mood hadn't changed a bit.

Fourteen

ONE THING THAT could go a long way toward changing Martin's mood was clearing things up with Hazeline. He hated thinking about her being mad at him, so he tried not to think about it. But a thought that big was hard to get rid of.

He dreaded and looked forward to Sunday. Dreaded having to see Hazeline, but looked forward to getting it over with. He hadn't realized how much he counted on Hazeline to be on his side. Maybe she wouldn't be anymore, after he'd let her down like that, standing there like a bump on a log, not taking up for himself.

Sunday morning, he got dressed and tiptoed into the

kitchen. He didn't want to wake his father up. He just wanted to get out of the trailer and be alone with Hazeline.

"Mornin'," his mother said, coming in the door. "It's hot as Hades out there. I don't think them tomato plants are gonna make it. They're just shriveling right up." She set two flowerpots on the kitchen counter. "Look at these pots I got at the flea market. Brand-new, and only fifty cents."

"Did Hazeline call?" Martin poured himself a glass of cold buttermilk.

"No. She supposed to?"

"Naw. I just wondered if she was still coming, is all."

"Why wouldn't she?"

"I don't know. Just asking." He tried to act casual as he buttered his toast. He scooped on a mound of peach preserves and hummed softly.

His mother sat on a stool behind the counter. He felt her eyes on him but he kept spreading and humming.

"Martin," she finally said, "Hazeline's not mad at you."

"I know." His eyes darted around for something to look at. He was relieved to hear Hazeline's car pull up. He nearly tripped on his untied shoelaces as he raced for the door, carrying his toast with him.

"See you," he called and jumped off the front steps just as Hazeline got out of the car.

"Well, hey," she said. "Either you're glad to see me or you're starving."

Martin tried to find a hint of anger in her voice, a twinge of disgust, a trace of meanness, but there was nothing. Just Hazeline being Hazeline, same as ever.

"Both," he said, stuffing the last of the toast into his mouth and licking his fingers. "I hope they have corn on the cob today, don't you?"

He hopped in the front seat, leaving Hazeline standing by the car. She got in and started the engine.

"Okay," she said, driving out of the trailer park. "What's wrong?"

"Nothing." Martin played the drums on the dashboard with his hands.

"How come you were in such a hurry to get out of there?"

"No reason."

"Martin Edward Pittman, don't lie to me. Why you acting so funny?"

He quit playing the drums. "I can't stand you being mad at me, Hazeline."

She slowed the car down, pulled off the road, and turned the ignition off. She turned to face him, leaning her back against the door, her arm draped over the back of the seat. He forced himself to look at her—a quick little sideways glance. What he saw brought him instant relief. Her face was a mixed-up crazy quilt of things, but all of them were good. Affection. Kindness. Even a hint of amusement. Finally she spoke.

"I ain't mad at you, Martin," she said. He wanted to hug her, but Hazeline had never been much for hugging. "When I saw you just standing there, letting your daddy say them things to you and you not uttering one word in your own defense, I felt a lot of things, but mad wasn't one of 'em. Peeved is more like it. Peeved at Ed, of course, but that's nothing new, and so peeved at you I wanted to snatch you bald-headed."

Martin wasn't sure how far removed peeved was from mad, but he felt better anyway.

"You gonna keep running from yourself, Martin?" she said.

He looked out the window. A bent-up hubcap was half hidden in the weeds. It glistened in the sun like some kind of lost treasure.

"You know, you can't change your daddy any more than he can change you," Hazeline said.

Martin kept staring at that glistening hubcap. "So why's he always trying to change me?"

"I wish I knew, Martin. Seems like I've spent half my life trying to figure out why he does anything. I never told you this before, but when I found out I was going to have your daddy, it kind of took me by surprise. Hell, I'd still be looking for babies under cabbage leaves if he hadn't come along and set me straight. That was over thirty years ago, and he's still surprising me." She lit a cigarette and blew a stream of smoke up in the air. It hovered at the roof of the car like a swirling gray cloud.

"Maybe if his daddy came back, he wouldn't be so mad all the time," Martin said.

Hazeline laughed so hard tears ran down her cheeks. Martin felt foolish. He crossed his arms and looked out the window.

"I'm sorry, sweetheart." Hazeline cupped his chin in her

hand and turned his face toward her. "You might have a point there."

"I want that violin, Hazeline."

"You want a hell of a lot more than that, Martin."

He nodded. He wanted his father to let him be what he wanted to be—and still like him. "Well, how am I going to get what I want, Hazeline?"

"If you're looking to me for answers, Martin, I can't give you any." She started the car and drove on.

"Do you think Wylene's crazy?" Martin asked as Hazeline turned the big Studebaker into the Howard Johnson's parking lot.

She smiled. Her leathery face wrinkled up in every imaginable place. "I think Wylene knows a good soul when she sees one." She patted Martin's knee. "Ain't nothing crazy about that, now, is there?"

Martin smiled back. "I sure hope they have corn on the cob," he said. "Don't you?"

Fifteen

IF MARTIN HAD to name the time of year he liked best, right down to the hour, it would have to be noon in July. Anyone who hasn't spent any time on an asphalt road in South Carolina at noon in July could never appreciate just how unusual a liking that was. But to Martin, noon in July was the time he had the whole world to himself. Leastways, he felt like he did. At noon in July in South Carolina, people scurry into air-conditioned houses, fan themselves on covered porches, nap in folding lounge chairs in the shade, and drink ice-cold beer in dark, smoky bars.

This particular July was especially hot and muggy, which meant the air-conditioned movie theater across the street from J. H. Lawrence and Son Pawnshop was especially crowded. That made it harder for Martin to find a comfortable place to stand. He'd been coming here every few days. He had tried to stay away, but it was impossible. When his feet started walking, they just took over and carried him right to Pickens, right to the movie theater across from the pawnshop. But once his feet got him that far, they wouldn't budge another inch. No matter how hard he tried, Martin couldn't make himself cross the street.

His no-worry week had come and gone. He had lost the ten dollars. His leather pouch was practically empty now, but it had been worth it to have one whole week knowing for sure the violin would still be there. He had considered talking to Mr. Lawrence again, but what would he say? He didn't have another ten dollars. He couldn't expect the man to hold the violin for nothing. Martin had convinced himself no one was going to buy it—ever. It was just going to lie there, nestled among the radios and watches, and wait for the day he walked in and claimed it. But in the meantime, every few days Martin found himself standing on the sidewalk at noon in July—watching.

"Why you going to Pickens so much?" his mother asked one day. She was sitting at a card table working a jigsaw puzzle: the Smoky Mountains cut up into about a million pieces. Her hand hovered over the pieces while her eyes searched.

"Just feel like it," Martin said.

He watched her and wondered if she was even thinking about the violin.

"Why don't you see if T.J. wants to go to a movie?" she said. "I'll drive ya'll in."

"Naw."

"Alma Scoggins wants you to cut some tree branches that's scraping the top of her trailer. Why don't you go on and do that now?"

"I'll do it later."

His mother looked up from her jigsaw puzzle and sighed. "Hazeline called. She wanted to know what we were going to do for your birthday. I thought maybe we could go out for pizza and miniature golf. How's that sound?"

"That'd be okay." Martin got a soda out of the refrigerator and watched his mother searching through the puzzle pieces.

"I still can't believe you're going to be thirteen," she said.

As far back as Martin could remember, his mother had said that. "I can't believe you're going to be eight . . . I can't believe you're going to be ten."

"I think I'll ride my bike into Pickens, okay?" Martin said.

"Oh, Martin, it's so hot."

"I don't care. It don't bother me."

"One of these days you're going to have a heatstroke out there."

Martin finished his soda and set off for Pickens. It was quiet in Paradise. Terry Lynn and Luke Scoggins splashed in a wading pool. A TV was on somewhere. But mostly it had that noon-in-July feel to it.

It was a sunny day, but the smell of rain was in the air. Sure enough, just as Martin got to Pickens, there was a sudden downpour. One of those quick thundershowers that was over almost as soon as it started. Puddles glittered in the sun, and rain-soaked Queen Anne's lace bowed over the roadside. Everything looked clean and fresh and steamy.

Martin walked his bike down the sidewalk. Under the store awnings, the pavement was cool and wet. By instinct, Martin looked up as he neared the movie theater, then stopped suddenly. His throat squeezed up tight. His whole body went stiff. He felt it even before he saw it. The violin was gone. The watches were there, the diamond rings, the dented television. But right in the middle was an empty space so big it nearly killed him.

For the longest time, Martin stood there, looking at that empty space. Finally he crossed the street. Maybe he was wrong. Maybe his eyes were playing tricks on him. When he got closer, he'd see that the violin was there, had been there all along. But when he got to the window and pressed his face against the glass, that empty space was bigger than ever.

Martin dropped his bike and pushed the door open so fast it hit the wall with a crash. Mr. Lawrence looked up from his newspaper.

"Where's the violin?" Martin demanded, willing his voice to be calm. Mr. Lawrence was going to say he'd just moved it. That it was over there, in a box, on a shelf, under a table. Anywhere but gone.

"Gone," Mr. Lawrence said so matter-of-factly Martin hated him for it.

"What do you mean, gone?"

"Gone. As in 'not here.' " Mr. Lawrence looked back at his newspaper. Martin wanted to snatch it out of his hands. To shake him. Make him say he was lying.

"Gone where?" Martin said.

"Sold."

"To who?"

"I don't know." Mr. Lawrence kept his eyes on the paper.

"Well, what'd they look like?" Martin could hear the panic in his voice. He took a deep breath. "I mean, was it a man or a woman?"

Mr. Lawrence looked up, an annoyed look on his face. When he spoke, his voice matched his face. "I don't think that's any of your business, son."

Martin felt like he'd been slapped.

"But if it's that all-fired important to you," Mr. Lawrence continued, "it was a woman."

Martin couldn't stop now. "What'd she look like?"

Mr. Lawrence chuckled and shook his head. "You don't give up, do you? Well, let's see. She was short. Bottle blonde. Skinny legs. Not your usual violin type, if you know what I mean."

Martin had no idea what your usual violin type was.

"Did you get her name?"

"No reason to."

"Did she write a check or anything?"

"Cash only." He pointed to a sign behind the counter.

Martin's mind raced. Who could she be? He'd seen short blond women with skinny legs, but he was pretty sure he didn't know any by name. And so what if he did know her? What good would that do? It didn't matter who the woman was. The violin was gone.

Martin felt so heavy he could barely stand up straight.

"I guess I'll be seeing you, then," he said, moving slowly toward the door. When he reached it, he was suddenly overcome with sadness. Not just for the lost violin but for leaving the shop for what he guessed would be the last time. Saying a final goodbye to Mr. Lawrence. He hadn't even liked the man, yet here he was feeling bad about saying goodbye.

Outside again, Martin squinted in the bright sunlight. He pedaled toward home and thought about missing something he had never owned, hadn't even come close to owning. He'd only held the violin once. But it had set the ball rolling for a heap of thoughts to come tumbling into his head that had never been there before. Or then again, maybe they had been there all along and he just hadn't noticed.

He rode by Sybil's house three times before she came out.

"I got something for you," she called through the screen door.

He pedaled up to her front porch.

"What?"

She disappeared inside. Martin waited. Was he supposed to follow her in? He peered through the screen. It was dark in the hall, and he could smell vinegar.

"Sybil?" He lifted one foot and pulled his sock up, then ran his hand over his hair.

Her head appeared around a doorway. "You coming in or what?"

Martin stepped into the hall. It was hot and damp inside and the vinegar fumes made his nose wrinkle up. "Hoo-eee," he said, waving a hand in front of his face.

He went to the kitchen where Sybil was. Glass jars covered the table and lined the countertops. Steam rose up out of a huge pot on the stove. Sybil's hair was damp and limp around her face.

She handed Martin a jar. "Pickled okra."

"You make these?" he said.

"Yeah." And then cool, calm Sybil blushed. Martin looked away quickly, pretending to examine the rows of jars around the room. "Thanks," he said. "Well, I guess I better go."

But instead of walking out the door, he just stood there in that hot, vinegary kitchen.

Sybil brushed her hair out of her face. "Maybe we could go fishing sometime," she said.

"Yeah, sure. We could do that."

"Course, we'd have to find us a better fishing spot than that lousy ole lake."

For a second, Martin felt ashamed. But when he looked up and saw Sybil's smile, that bad feeling passed. He smiled back.

"Well, I guess I better go," he said again. This time he forced his feet to take him outside, where he tucked the still-warm jar inside his shirt and pedaled off.

At the highway, he turned left, away from Paradise Trailer Park. He wasn't ready to go home just yet. He pedaled slowly, steadily. The rhythmic whirring of the wheels was almost hypnotic. He tried to hum a tune instead of thinking about the violin. He picked up speed as he coasted downhill and onto Walhalla Highway. When he saw the Exxon station just ahead, he spotted Frank right away, rolling a tire out to a pickup truck. Same thin, brown arms. Same ponytail. Same crinkly-eyed smile.

Martin kept his head down and focused on the road as it whizzed under the front wheel of his bike. He wished he could pull in and say "Hi." Wished he could wave. Shout out a friendly "Hey, Frank!"

Within seconds the gas station was behind him and he was still pedaling and thinking and wishing. Then he stopped so suddenly the wheels of his bike skidded in the dirt along the roadside. He turned around and rode back toward the gas station.

"Hey, Frank," he called, waving a hand over his head.

Frank looked up. He squinted in Martin's direction, then grinned and waved.

When the gas station was far behind him, Martin pumped his fist in the air and said, "Yes!" Then he put his hand on the warm jar of okra and headed for home.

Sixteen

Neither Martin nor Wylene had mentioned the violin in days. Finally, one day out of the clear blue, Wylene said, "You seen that violin lately?"

She was cleaning around her kitchen sink with a toothbrush, scrubbing away invisible particles of mildew from around the faucet. She was wearing a Hawaiian-print muumuu and yellow rubber gloves that came up to her elbows. Martin sat on the floor in the living room eating a Popsicle. They were listening to Vivaldi. Violin concertos.

"Nope," Martin said. "It ain't there."

Wylene stopped scrubbing and came into the living room. "Ain't there?"

"Nope."

"What happened to it?"

"Some blond woman bought it." The Popsicle was melting as quick as he could eat it. Purple juice ran down his arms and dripped off his elbows. He went to get some paper towels and finish eating over the sink. Wylene followed him.

"What're you gonna do now?" she asked.

"Nothing much I can do."

"Well, that's a crying shame, Martin. I just feel terrible."

Martin nodded, but he knew there was no way she could feel half as terrible as he did. Wasn't he the one who had spent all those weeks seeing himself playing that violin? Hadn't he heard the music, felt the smooth wood in his hands, moved the bow across the strings? He'd pictured himself playing in the little living room of his trailer. Mamma, Daddy, Hazeline all sitting on the couch smiling, asking him to play more. Then in one big swoop all that had disappeared and he was right back into real life again.

The summer seemed endless now, one long day following another. Southern summers are long. Not like winters; they just come in the front door and go right out the back door without so much as a 'How do you do?' in between. But summers come in and stay awhile.

On Martin's birthday, Hazeline came over and they all went out for pizza and miniature golf. Afterward they sat on lawn chairs in front of the trailer, eating homemade peach ice cream and swatting mosquitoes. Martin's mother invited the Scogginses over. Terry Lynn and Luke brought sparklers.

Alma Scoggins had a way about her that attracted people. Her loud, happy voice always sounded like something special was going on, some event that made people gather around. She'd send Mr. Scoggins into the rickety shed behind their trailer for more chairs. Terry Lynn and Luke would race each other to fetch more Dixie cups or chips. So before long, with Mrs. Scoggins there, a regular crowd sat around drinking sodas and watching Martin open presents. A denim jacket from his mother and father. Sneakers from Hazeline. A Randy Travis tape from T.J.

Mrs. Scoggins bustled around making sure everyone had enough to eat and drink. "Now you got to tell us, Martin," she said. "How does it feel to be thirteen? You don't look no different."

"Feels about the same, I reckon," Martin said.

"How come Wylene don't never come out?" Mrs. Scoggins asked nobody in particular. A couple people shrugged their shoulders, but nobody answered. "That woman's going to wither up and die locked up in that trailer like that," Mrs. Scoggins went on.

Mr. Pittman laughed. "Well now, that'd be a sad day in Paradise, wouldn't it?" he said.

Mrs. Scoggins flapped her hand in his direction and turned to Martin. "Go on down there and get her, Martin. She might like some of this ice cream."

Martin felt people looking at him. He watched Luke

Scoggins swirling a sparkler around in a figure eight until it fizzled out.

"Naw," he finally said. "I don't think she'd want to come. Too many mosquitoes out here."

"Oh, for crying out loud," Mrs. Scoggins said.

Martin's mother laughed. "Alma, you might as well give up trying to get Wylene Lundsford out of that trailer," she said.

"Well, I think it's just pitiful the way she acts. She must be plum damn miserable in there."

There was a rumble of thunder, and heat lightning lit up the sky. One by one everybody drifted back to their trailers.

"I better be gettin', too," said Hazeline. "See ya'll Sunday."

She gave Martin a peck on the cheek and drove off in a cloud of dust.

As soon as his father went inside, Martin said, "I'm going to Wylene's." He tried to act casual as he folded up chairs.

"Kind of late, isn't it?" his mother asked, stuffing paper plates into a garbage bag.

"I won't stay long. She asked me to stop by for a minute." Martin looked around the yard strewn with paper cups and wrapping paper. "Thanks for all this, Mamma," he added.

Wylene's trailer was quiet. If her porch light hadn't been on, Martin would've thought she'd already gone to bed. He was halfway up the walk when she greeted him from the door.

"Happy birthday," she called. She had on her muumuu. Her hair was curled and stiff with hair spray.

"Thanks. Kinda quiet in here," Martin said. "How come no music?"

"I don't know. I guess I was just enjoying the night sounds. I love to hear crickets, don't you?"

Martin went inside. "The Lord's choir, Hazeline calls 'em," he said.

Wylene came out of the kitchen carrying a cake and sang "Happy Birthday" to him. She cut them each a thick slice. Red velvet. His favorite.

"Pretty good if I do say so myself," she said.

"Mmmm," Martin mumbled, his mouth full.

"I'll be right back." Wylene disappeared into the bedroom and came back with a box wrapped in the Sunday comics and tied with yarn.

"Thanks." Martin held the gift to his ear and shook it. Wylene watched, grinning.

"Go ahead. Open it."

Martin tore off the paper. He looked down at the portable tape player in his hand. "This is real nice, Wylene."

"Listen to it." Wylene took the earphones out of his hand and put them in his ears. She pressed the PLAY button.

Beethoven's Ninth Symphony blasted into Martin's ears. He jumped, then grinned up at her. "Thanks," he yelled over the music. Taking the earphones out of his ears, he repeated, "Thanks," more quietly.

Wylene giggled. "Now you can listen to music anytime. Can't nobody hear but you. Now I got another surprise." She hurried out of the room again.

"Close your eyes," she called out in a singsongy voice.

"Okay, they're closed."

"Don't peek."

Her muumuu rustled as she walked back into the room. She put something on the coffee table in front of him.

"Okay, you can look now."

Martin opened his eyes. It took a minute for his eyes and his brain to connect. To realize exactly what he was looking at. His violin. He knew right away it was the one from the pawnshop. Same smooth, polished wood. Same curved sides. Same curling neck. If he had been alone, he would have grabbed it. Hugged it. Maybe even kissed it.

"Well," Wylene said. "How d'you like it?"

Martin looked at her, then back at the violin, back at Wylene.

She laughed. "That blond woman was Donna Reese. From out at the plant? You know." She waved a freckled hand. "I met her on second shift? Well, you know how much I hate going in places I never been before, and Donna goes into Pickens all the time and knew right where that pawnshop was, so I asked her to get it for me. It never even dawned on me you'd go in there and find out who bought it. I like to died when you told me about a blond woman."

"I can't take this, Wylene."

"Of course you can't. 'Cause it ain't yours," she said. "It's mine."

Martin stared up at her, trying to understand what she was saying.

"But you can play it any time you want to," she said, winking.

Martin looked at the violin. It looked strange and out of place sitting there on Wylene's coffee table.

"Don't you want to try it?" Wylene said.

"I don't know," he said softly.

"You don't know?" Wylene's voice was shrill. "For crying out loud, Martin, try it!"

"I don't know how to play a violin, Wylene."

She looked hurt. She sat down in the La-Z-Boy. The two of them just sat there looking at the violin, listening to the crickets.

Then Martin stood up. He reached out and slowly picked up the violin. It felt solid, warm. He put it under his chin and wished he was alone. He closed his eyes for a minute. He picked up the bow, unsure about how to hold it, trying several ways until it felt comfortable. As he put the bow on the strings, Wylene leaned forward. Martin's stomach twisted up into a knot. His elbow jutted out awkwardly. He closed his eyes again, held his breath, and moved the bow across the strings.

A shrill, squawking noise filled the trailer. Martin looked at Wylene. They both burst into laughter. Wylene rocked back and forth, wiping her eyes and laughing like Martin had never seen her laugh before. He held the violin and bow at his side and laughed with her, a good, tension-breaking laugh. After a minute, the laughter died and they were quiet. Martin lifted the violin to his chin again. Once more he pushed the bow across the strings.

Another shrill, squawking noise. But this time they didn't laugh. He moved the bow again, bending his elbow and pushing the bow in toward him, then straightening his arm out as he pulled it over the strings. Then again, and again. Each time the sound was raspy and squeaky. Martin tried holding the bow a little lighter against the strings and noticed the sound was not as loud. He angled the bow away from him and then toward him, noting how the sound was different each time. And in the middle of his experimenting, suddenly, unexpectedly, there was a clear, rich tone, just one note, sounding out sure and perfect. Martin looked at Wylene and raised his eyebrows. She smiled and nodded her head at him to go on. He moved the bow up again. An okay note, not as good as the one before, but better than the first ones. Then he pulled the bow down. Again a rich, sweet tone. The sound filled the trailer like the smell of baking bread, wrapping itself around Martin. Wylene disappeared. The crickets disappeared.

Martin kept moving the bow back and forth, back and forth, over the strings. The violin seemed to become warmer, to melt right into his shoulder. The bow became part of his hand. Note after note was clear-sounding, with only a few screechy ones now and then. It wasn't a song, a piece of music you could put a name to, but it was music all the same.

Martin had no idea how long he played. When he finally stopped, he stood there, still holding the violin under his chin, the bow resting lightly on the strings. Wylene's soft whisper broke the silence.

"It's a miracle," she said, so softly he barely heard her. "Martin Pittman, you are a musical miracle," she said a little louder. "I do declare I think Mr. Ludwig van Beethoven has come back to life right here in Paradise."

She began to laugh: a low, soft chuckle that grew until it was a downright whoop.

"I really am in Paradise!" She raced around the room excitedly, slamming down windows.

"What are you doing?" Martin said, watching her disappear into the bedroom. Windows slammed. She reappeared. Was she crazy, closing up the trailer like that in this heat?

"I got a secret to keep," she told him excitedly. Martin just stared at her.

"I got my own private Beethoven," she said, "and ain't no nosy damn neighbor gonna mess this up." She beamed at Martin. "Now, Mr. Beethoven," she said, "play."

Seventeen

MARTIN HAD KNOWN some happy times in his life, but none of them compared to the days that followed. If he could have changed anything about those days, he would have made them longer. The only bad part was waiting for Wylene to get home from work. To make time go faster, Martin stayed busy. He mowed lawns, did chores for Mrs. Scoggins, washed Hazeline's car. He even played catch with T.J. once or twice. But as soon as Wylene's car turned in to Paradise, Martin's heart raced, his stomach knotted, and he could barely keep his feet from running over to the tidy little trailer with the real front steps.

"What's wrong with you, anyway?" T.J. asked one day.

"What do you mean?" Martin said.

"I mean, how come you're always about to bust a gut to get over to Wylene's?"

"I ain't always about to bust a gut to get over to Wylene's."

"Yeah, you are."

"You're crazy," Martin said.

"Ya'll sure must like that Beethoven stuff."

Martin's heart dropped into his stomach. Had T.J. heard the violin? "Ain't no law against that, is there?" he said.

T.J. grinned and winked at Martin. "Seems to me like you two got something going on," he said.

"Shut up, T.J.," Martin said. His voice sounded irritated, but on the inside he was scared.

"Aw, hell, Martin, it don't matter to me. Just seems kind of weird is all. She's about as old as my mamma."

"Look, T.J.," Martin said. "Me and Wylene are just friends. I give up a long time ago trying to make people understand that. If you or Riley or anybody else's got a problem with that, then tough. Ain't nothing I can do about that, okay?"

"Okay with me." T.J. shrugged. And that was the end of it—at least for that day.

Every minute Martin spent at Wylene's was something to be savored. At first he practiced just running the bow across the four strings. Then he experimented with placing his fingers on the neck of the violin. If he pressed the tip of his finger on one of the strings, no matter which string it was, the note would be higher than that string just played alone. He tried positioning two fingers on the strings, then three. Just like he'd figured out patterns when he was learning to play the harmonica, he was beginning to see patterns in making different notes on the violin.

Next he tried combinations of notes, playing some faster than others, holding some notes out for a long time, others barely at all. Minutes, hours, days went by, and those clusters of slow and fast notes started to sound like tunes. He tried copying tunes he'd heard before, moving his fingers around until he figured out just where they needed to go and how long each note needed to be held. Then he tried making up tunes of his own. It was getting so that most of the time he hardly even noticed the bow moving back and forth, and only had to think of what he wanted a note to sound like for his fingers to make it happen. He only concentrated on the music, all the feelings he never talked about swirling around in notes, coming out of the violin like magic.

Sometimes Wylene would putter around the trailer while Martin played. Other times she just sat in the La-Z-Boy with her eyes closed, a little smile on her face. Every now and then she hummed along. Anyone who walked into that trailer on one of those hot summer days would have had a hard time figuring which one was happier, Martin or Wylene.

But as sure as rain in April, a secret didn't stay a secret for long in Paradise Trailer Park. When people are all jammed up together like bees in a hive, it's only natural they get to know one another pretty well. Who lost a job. Who drank too much. Who was getting a divorce, having a baby, going to nursing school. And whatever little nugget of knowledge was found was shared—quickly and eagerly.

Martin had lived in trailer parks all his life, so it came as no surprise when his mother said to him, "Martin, what's going on at Wylene's?" Still, he managed to put a look of surprise on his face.

"What do you mean?"

"Mildred Dennis says you been spending an awful lot of time over there. I thought you were cutting lawns over in Pickens."

"I am." Martin was glad that was the truth. "I been going to Wylene's after that, is all. She got some new tapes."

His mother's face was drawn and tight. She cocked her head and eyed Martin. "How come ya'll close the place up like that in this heat?" she asked.

Martin shifted his weight from one foot to the other. "I reckon she just likes it like that," he said. He might as well have said, "I'm telling you a big, fat, whopping lie."

"I don't know what you're up to, Martin, but your daddy's starting to notice something funny going on. He's already said a couple of things to me, and if you were around here long enough, he'd be saying 'em to you."

"Like what?"

"Like what in tarnation are you doing over at Wylene's every dern minute of the day."

"Maybe it's better than being here." Martin jammed the toe of his sneaker into the floor.

"Martin, all I'm saying is this. You're entitled to some privacy in your life. I know it's hard cooped up in this trailer park all the time. But if you're doing something your daddy'd disapprove of, I hope you'll think twice about it. Spare us both a little heartache maybe. You hear what I'm saying?"

Okay, he'd been warned. But that wasn't going to change anything. Wasn't going to stop him from going to Wylene's. Couldn't make him stop playing the violin. It would take a heck of a lot more than a warning to do that.

That afternoon Martin rode his bike for a while just to kill some time until Wylene got home. He loved his new tape player. He still liked to sing or listen to music in his head, but it was fun to listen to real music once in a while, too. Over and over again he listened to Beethoven's Sonata No. 9 in A Major. He had no idea what "A Major" was, but he thought he could figure it out if he listened enough.

When he got back to Paradise, he was sorry to see Riley sitting in front of the Owenses' trailer. He was looking at a motorcycle magazine, his feet propped up on a rusty barbecue grill. The patch of dirt that passed for a yard was littered with cinder blocks and old tires. A bicycle with only one wheel. Plastic flowerpots with nothing but dirt in them.

"Hey, what's happ'nin'," Riley called.

"Not much." Martin kept pedaling.

"I tell you what, Armpit," Riley said loudly, "you sure got everybody in this hellhole talkin' about you."

Martin stopped. Okay, he'd take the bait.

"How come?" he said.

Riley grinned and winked. "Like you don't know," he said.

"Why don't you just tell me and save us both some time, Riley. I got things to do."

"Aw, now, Armpit. Don't be shy. You can tell your ole pal Riley."

Martin started walking his bike toward home.

"The love nest, Armpit. I'm talking about the love nest," Riley called after him.

Martin's face burned. He walked slowly back to where Riley sat. He had never liked Riley, but now he was beginning to hate him. Full-blown, all-out, no-doubt-about-it hate. He glared down at Riley. "I don't really give a damn what you or anybody else thinks about what I do."

"Hey, I ain't knockin' it. I think it's kind of cute," Riley said.

Martin headed toward home again. He almost wished Riley would call out to him again because he'd already decided not to give him the satisfaction of a reply. But this time Riley kept quiet except for a laugh, and Martin kept going.

He had a lot of mixed up feelings tumbling around inside him. Ever since that first night at Wylene's, playing the violin, Martin felt like he was doing just what he was supposed to be doing. But mixed in with that good feeling was this other feeling that wasn't so good, a feeling that nagged at him and made him ask himself, "If I'm doing what I'm supposed to be doing, then how come I'm keeping it a secret?"

Eighteen

THE DAY SYBIL showed up at Paradise Trailer Park was about the hottest day anyone in Six Mile, South Carolina, could remember. The trailer park was quiet and deserted except for a couple of dogs sleeping in the shade and the Scoggins kids playing with the hose.

Martin sat on the front steps listening to his tape player, slapping his knees with both hands. He didn't notice Sybil until she tapped him lightly on the shoulder. She looked so out of place standing there in front of his trailer that for a minute he forgot where he was.

She pulled one earphone away from his ear, leaned down, and said, "Hey," right in his ear.

He took the earphones off and stood up.

"Hey, yourself."

"I brought you these." She held out a paper bag. She wore her bangly bracelets and a T-shirt that said: "My Mom Went to Disney World and All I Got Was This Dumb T-shirt." She thrust the bag at him.

He looked inside. Tomatoes. "Thanks," he said.

"Well, see ya." She turned to go. Her bicycle lay on its side at the edge of the road.

"Wait!" Martin called, but when she stopped and faced him, he didn't know what to say next. She waited. Sybil-so-patient. Sybil-so-cool.

"I want to show you something," Martin said.

"What?"

"Uh, it's not here. I mean, it's somewhere else."

"Where?"

"I'll show you."

He led her up the gravel road toward Wylene's. Please be home, he prayed.

When he heard the twang of the radio drifting from Wylene's trailer, he looked at Sybil and smiled.

"Where are we going?" she asked.

"You'll see." Martin knocked on Wylene's screen door so hard it banged and rattled against the trailer.

"Hold your horses," Wylene called from the kitchen.

Her flip-flops slapped against the bottom of her feet as she walked to the door.

"Well, hey there," she said. Her eyes darted nervously to Sybil, then back at Martin.

"This is Sybil," Martin said.

Wylene held the door open for them. "This place is a pigsty. It's just too dern hot to do anything. I almost wish I had to work tonight so I could be in the air-conditioning. You all want something cold to drink? I got soda and lemonade."

Martin recognized her fast, run-together nervous talk.

She turned the radio off and flip-flopped into the kitchen. She kept shooting quick little glances at Sybil.

"Sybil just moved to Six Mile," Martin said. "She has a garden."

Wylene's face relaxed a little. "Oh, I just love gardening. I wish I had a good spot for one, but it's too shady here." She plunked ice into three glasses and poured soda into them. One of them overflowed onto the counter.

Martin wondered why Sybil was being so quiet. Then he remembered the way she had been that first day at school: looking everyone over; sizing them up.

Finally she said, "I bet you could grow lettuce."

"You think so?" Wylene handed them a drink and flip-flopped back into the living room. She had on shorts. Her legs were white and plump and freckled.

"I thought I'd show Sybil your violin," Martin said.

"Oh." Wylene looked at Martin wide-eyed. She brushed invisible crumbs from the coffee table, fluffed the pillows on the couch. "Well, sure, okay."

She brought the violin out from the bedroom and held it up for Sybil to see.

"That's nice," Sybil said. "Is it hard to play?"

"Oh, I don't play it." Wylene chuckled. "Martin plays it."

Sybil looked at Martin, and for a minute he wished he hadn't done this. But it was too late now, so he said, "Well, not very good."

"Not very good?" Wylene shrieked. She turned to Sybil and said, "Martin has a gift. Like Beethoven."

Sybil turned her slow gaze to Martin. "Play something," she said.

"What?"

"I don't know. Anything."

Martin realized he was still holding the bag of tomatoes, now damp and wrinkled in his hand. Sybil took the bag from him and sat on the edge of the couch.

Martin took the violin from Wylene and placed it gently under his chin. Wylene shut the front door and sat in the La-Z-Boy. Martin knew that if he didn't start playing right away he'd never be able to, so he moved the bow slowly across the strings, just making notes at first. Then he closed his eyes and let the notes run together, one after the other, until he drifted away into the music.

Later, when Martin and Sybil sat by their bikes at the edge of the lake and he told her about how he had wanted the violin but his father wouldn't let him have it and how Wylene had bought it and all that, she just watched him with those cool, cool eyes.

Then she stood up and skimmed a stone across the top of the lake. It bounced three times, leaving a trail of ripples on the surface of the muddy water.

"Well, I guess a person's got to handle things their own way," she said, taking another stone out of the pocket of her cutoffs.

What was that supposed to mean? Martin watched her bracelets dance up and down her arm as she threw another stone. She sat back down and gave Martin a look that made him feel like a little kid being scolded. He flushed. What did she know about anything? When was the last time her smiling daddy had yelled or thrown anything or made her feel like a piece of dirt for breathing the wrong way?

"I never should have taken you to Wylene's." His voice was shaky. He cleared his throat and forced himself to look at her. She looked back at him with that confident look of hers.

"I'm not sure who it is you're mad at, Martin," she said.

Now, that took him by surprise. He looked out at the water and then down at his feet. The toes of his sneakers were wet and muddy. His ankles were dotted with bumpy, red mosquito bites.

Sybil stood up and brushed off the seat of her jeans. "I better head on back. My dad and I are going out for Chinese food tonight."

Martin was glad she had changed the subject. He was confused and uncomfortable, and right now those were two feelings he wasn't in the mood for.

They rode silently down the dirt road. When they got to the highway, they turned in opposite directions.

"Thanks for the tomatoes," he called after her. She waved a hand over her head. Her bracelets glistened in the sun.

Martin watched her until she disappeared from view. He wished he was going with her. Wished he was going home with her to stand out in the garden and look at okra and play the violin and not be mad at whoever it was he was mad at.

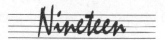

Nineteen

"YOUR FRIEND SYBIL'S here," Martin's mother called from the living room.

Martin stared at himself in the dresser mirror, his mouth hanging open and his eyes wide. Sybil? Here? In his trailer?

"Coming," he called. He smoothed his hair down with his hand and composed his face in the mirror before going out to greet her.

She sat on the sofa across from Martin's father. Her legs were crossed, one foot bouncing up and down as she talked. She clutched a paper bag in her lap.

". . . moved in with my dad when my mother went to Texas," she was saying to Martin's parents.

She looked up when Martin came in the room. Her eyes showed a hint of amusement that irritated Martin. She held up the bag, those bangly bracelets sliding down to her elbow. "Green beans," she said.

Martin's mother took the bag and peered inside. "Are these from your garden?" she asked.

"Yes, ma'am," Sybil said.

"That's mighty nice of you, Sybil," Martin's father said. He pushed the recliner back and took a sip of coffee. "Nothing like homegrown. You have a big garden?"

"Not as big as I'd like. Next year I'm going to make it bigger." She smiled at Martin. He looked away, watching his mother put the beans in the refrigerator.

"I've thought about planting some weeds out there just to give myself something else to do." Sybil laughed. Martin's father laughed. Martin walked to the front door and stared out at nothing in particular, wondering why he was feeling so uncomfortable.

"You say your daddy works down at the Exxon?" Martin's father said.

"Yessir."

"Maybe he could get me a deal on some tires."

"You could ask him," Sybil said. "I'm sure he wouldn't mind. He's just crazy about Martin, you know."

Martin felt that familiar ball in the pit of his stomach. In his mind he saw Frank and his father together. He tried to imagine them laughing, slapping each other's backs, making a deal on some tires. He looked over at Sybil, watched her chatting with his father like they were old friends. What was she doing mixing up her life with his, sitting here in his trailer talking about Frank? Then out of the clear blue she said, "You must be pretty proud of Martin."

"Oh?" his father said. "Why's that?"

Martin watched a sparrow splashing in a puddle in the front yard. He wished he was out there, too, splashing around. Then, when he'd had his fill of that muddy water, he'd up and just fly away. He heard Sybil stirring on the sofa, bracelets clanging.

"You know, his musical talent and all." Sybil used a surprised, you-oughtta-know-that kind of tone. Martin glanced at his father and saw the clenched jaw, the narrowing eyes.

"No," his father said, "I can't say that I'm particularly proud of that."

Martin watched Sybil's face change, her smile disappear, her own eyes narrow slightly. She cocked her head and tilted her chin up and said, "That's too bad." Her foot bounced harder, faster. "You ever listen to him play that harmonica? Me and my dad just can't get enough of it. Sometimes I nearly cry it sounds so pretty." She leaned forward and added, "And I'm not exactly the crying type."

Martin looked back out at the yard. The sparrow was gone.

"I bet if Martin got that violin he's been wanting, he could really play some nice music," Sybil said.

Martin's father slammed the recliner down with a bang

and Martin stepped between his father and Sybil. He grabbed her hand and pulled her toward the door.

"We're going to take a ride down to the lake," he said. Outside, he jumped on his bike and rode off in a swirl of dust. At the main road, he leaned forward and pedaled furiously. He stared down at the asphalt rushing beneath him and felt the sweat running down his back.

When he got to the lake, he threw his bike down and sat in the grass near the edge of the water. He didn't look up at the sound of Sybil's bike on the dirt road above him. Didn't move when she sat down beside him.

"You mad at me?" Sybil said.

Martin jumped up and turned to face her. He let out one little "Ha!" and started pacing, his sneakers making squishy noises in the wet mud at the water's edge. Finally he stopped and looked at her.

"Stay away from my family, Sybil." He struggled to catch his breath before continuing. "I don't need you to stir things up with my daddy. I can do that all by myself." He felt a flicker of pleasure when he noticed that Sybil's usually cool expression was gone. That her chin was quivering, her hands shaking.

She clutched her knees and stared out at the lake. "At least I'm not afraid of being myself," she said.

Martin stopped pacing and looked down at her. "What makes you think I am?"

When she looked up at him, her Sybil-cool expression had returned. "You got a violin hidden away up at Wylene's.

A violin you play like I never heard anybody play before. A violin you won't even bring into your own home."

"You don't know anything about me, Sybil," Martin said. His voice echoed across the still water. "You and your daddy living in your happy little world don't know anything. I ain't nothing to my daddy but a disappointment, and I hate him."

Martin turned away from Sybil and walked out into the water, kicking it over and over, sending splashes of muddy water into the air. He whirled around to face Sybil. "I wish my daddy was somebody like yours," he said. "Somebody I'd be glad to come home to, somebody who laughs just for the heck of it and treats me good. But he ain't. I wish I could be a fast-pitching baseball fool like T.J., but I ain't. And I could keep on wishing till kingdom come, but that ain't gonna make it happen." He kicked at the water again.

"You're mighty uppity, Martin, you know that?" Sybil said.

Martin threw his hands up and looked at the sky. There wasn't any use even commenting on that, coming from someone who had just sashayed into his home and tried to start something. Sybil hugged her knees and rocked back and forth.

"You think you're the only one on this planet who ever felt like that?" she said. "You think you got a patent on wishing people were different?"

"I never said that."

"You might as well have."

"I reckon you been wishing your daddy wasn't so nice, right?"

Sybil jumped up and put her hands on her hips. "You're as mean as your daddy," she said and sat back down so hard she let out an "oomph." She picked up a stone and threw it into the water. "I've done my share of wishing," she said. "But I'm a lot smarter now."

"Well, maybe I'm just a dumb ass, Sybil, okay?"

"Maybe you are," she said.

Martin sat down close to the water, feeling the wet seep through the seat of his jeans but not caring.

Sybil threw another stone. "You know, one time I got sick at school and the nurse called my house for someone to come get me," she said. "I waited in the nurse's office for my mom, but it was my dad that came walking in the door. He had grease plumb up to his elbows. Dirty old rags hanging out of his pockets. His shoes all caked with mud. I looked that nurse right in the eye and said, 'That ain't my dad.' "

Martin watched Sybil dig another rock out of the wet mud, waiting for her to go on. When she didn't, he said, "Then what happened?"

"My dad just turned around and walked out of the room."

Martin said, "Wow," and then felt foolish. Wished he hadn't said it.

"I was scared to death to go home that day," Sybil said. "But when I walked in the kitchen, my dad just handed me a peanut-butter-and-banana sandwich."

"What'd you do?" Martin said.

"I ate that sandwich and wished like anything I could have started that day all over again." Sybil wiped her muddy hands on the seat of her shorts. "But at least I saw a few things with new eyes."

She started up the hill toward her bike, then turned and looked down at Martin. "I feel sorry for you, Martin. You just keep looking through the same old eyes."

The sun behind her made a silhouette of her climbing on her bike and riding away. He stared down the empty road, thinking he was mad at Sybil for sitting in his trailer and talking to his daddy. Thinking she wasn't so damn cool after all. Thinking she was wrong about him and his same old eyes. He stood up and looked down at himself. His legs were wet and muddy. There was a squishy, sucking sound when he pulled his feet out of the mud one at a time. He thought about that sparrow he had seen in his yard. Thought about that sparrow flying away while he was still standing here in the mud. Then he kicked at the water and said "Shoot" before climbing on his bike and heading home.

Twenty

JULY HAD TURNED into August, and Martin could already feel summer drifting away. He couldn't quite put his finger on what made him feel that way. Surely not the weather, which was as hot and muggy as ever. He guessed it was just the little things. Kids coming home from town with brand-new backpacks. T.J. talking about football.

Martin wanted to hold on to summer as long as he could. Once school started, he wouldn't have nearly as much time for the violin.

Everything about it still felt new to him. Each time he picked it up felt as good as the very first time. The feel of the smooth wood under his chin. The slender, delicate neck beneath his fingers. The hardest part about holding it was putting it down again. It hadn't come with a case, but Wylene had found an old suitcase that was just the right size. She and Martin had cut foam rubber to line the bottom. Each time he finished playing, he polished off the fingerprints and blew away any little particles of dust that might have settled on the strings. Then he admired it one more time before returning it to its foam-rubber cradle.

Martin had developed a system for teaching himself to play. First he would sit on the floor of Wylene's trailer and listen to music. He would pick out a part he especially liked and listen to it over and over again. Then he would try to play it. And he kept on playing until he got the notes just right, the rhythm just right. When he felt like he had a piece down real good, he could begin to put his feelings into it. To make it his own. "Giving it that personal touch," Wylene called it.

"That's the sign of a true artist," she said. "Anybody can just copy something, but it takes an artist to make it special. I'm telling you, Martin, you got a gift."

One afternoon the two of them sat on the floor playing Chinese checkers and listening to the music from *The King and I.* The violin lay between them on the coffee table. Every now and then Martin ran his fingers up and down the strings or plucked along with the record. Wylene wagged her head from side to side and tapped her toes together. She was wearing madras Bermuda shorts. Her pudgy white legs stuck straight out in front of her. Even in the heat, she wore her fuzzy slippers. She looked down at the checkerboard, contemplating her next move and happily singing "Getting to Know You." Wylene hadn't had one of her bad days since the violin had come into their lives.

"I feel like I have a purpose now," she'd said.

Martin watched her waving her hands in the air, conducting an invisible orchestra. Every now and then she'd point at Martin and say, "Here's your part," and they'd stop the game to listen to the violin part. A fan whirred on the kitchen counter. The window shades were pulled down and the room was dark and kind of mysterious. Martin pretended that nothing outside the trailer existed, that they were floating around in space, high above the dirt-and-gravel world of Paradise Trailer Park.

"How about a Little Debbie snack cake?" Wylene said when they finished their game.

"Sure. That sounds good."

"Lemonade or soda?"

"Soda." Martin stayed on the floor, putting the marbles back in their container.

"Ain't it funny how you can't tell what time it is when you can't see outside?" Wylene opened ice trays over the sink. "I mean, it could be the middle of the night and you wouldn't even know it if you didn't have a clock." Martin watched her pour soda into the glasses. It foamed up to the top, fizzing. "What time you think it is now?" Wylene said. "Don't look."

Before Martin could answer, a noise invaded their floating trailer world. A knock on the door. Martin and Wylene froze: Wylene with the soda can stuck in midair, Martin on the floor, watching the soda can stuck in midair. Before either one of them could move, the door flew open and Martin's father stepped inside.

His presence in Wylene's trailer was so overwhelmingly strange, so undeniably foreign, that for the longest time Martin and Wylene just stared at Mr. Pittman. Martin was sure his heart had stopped beating.

It was Martin's father who broke the silence by letting the screen door bang shut behind him. Wylene backed up against the kitchen sink, still holding the can suspended in midair.

Martin watched his father's face, the squinty eyes, the stubbly growth of coarse black hair poking out of his chin. Their eyes met and then, at the exact same time, traveled down to the violin nestled in the suitcase on the coffee table.

Finally his father spoke. "Hello, Martin."

From his spot on the floor, Martin had to look up. His father loomed over him. Martin could see the hair in his nostrils, smell his sweat.

"I hope I ain't interruptin' anything," his father said. "You all havin' band practice in here today?"

When his father picked up the violin, Martin wanted to jump up and choke him. But while his insides were stewing around like a pot ready to boil over, his body just sat there, unable to move.

His father strummed the violin strings with his thumb. Four loud, ugly twangs.

"Martin," he said in a calm, quiet voice, "I suggest you kiss this thing goodbye and take it back to where you got it."

Martin heard the soda can slam down on the kitchen counter. "It ain't Martin's to take back, Mr. Pittman," Wylene said. "It's mine."

Mr. Pittman looked at her, and in that instant Martin realized that not once had his father and Wylene ever spoken to each other. He was mesmerized by the sight of it. And to top it off, there was scared-of-her-own-shadow Wylene standing there with her chin stuck up in the air and her hands on her hips, talking back to his father like she'd never been afraid of anything in her life.

His father smiled and chuckled silently, shaking his head and inspecting his fingernails before he spoke again.

"Well, Miss Lundsford, then I suggest you take this thing back to where you got it."

"I suggest you get the hell out of my trailer," she said.

"I'll do that," he said, pushing the screen door open. Then he turned back and said over his shoulder, "Nice meetin' you, Miss Lundsford," and disappeared into the brightness outside, taking the violin with him.

Twenty-one

FROM HIS SPOT on the floor, Martin watched Wylene's fuzzy slippers shuffle across the room. She sat down in the La-Z-Boy and dropped her face into her hands, sobbing loudly. Every few seconds she took a deep, gasping breath, lifting her shoulders and then letting them fall heavily.

Martin got up and left the trailer. He went down the real-not-cinder-block steps. Down the neat brick walk. Past the blue birdbath, the pecking hen, the row of chicks. He walked down the gravel road past the Owenses', past the Scogginses', and right up his own cinder-block steps into his trailer. His father sat on the couch staring at the TV.

Martin stood in the doorway and glared at his father. "Give me back the violin," he said.

His father kept his eyes on the TV.

"That violin ain't yours, Daddy." Martin felt his pulse pounding inside his head.

"Get out of here, boy," his father said in that calm-before-the-storm voice.

Laughter came from the TV set.

Martin's mother came in from the bedroom. She looked at Martin with wide eyes. "What's the matter?" she asked.

"Stay out of this, Doris," his father said.

Martin clenched his hands into fists and squeezed until his nails dug into his palms. "How come you got such a problem with that violin?"

He heard his own voice and for a minute was surprised that he was really saying the words and not just thinking them.

"I ain't got a problem with that violin," his father answered. "I got a problem with you."

"Then why don't you tell me what it is?"

"All right, I'll tell you." His father turned away from the TV and glared back at Martin. "I look at you and I hate what I see."

"What do you see?"

"I see you never doing nothing right. All my life I ain't never had nothing but disappointments, and you're just the icing on the cake."

"I know I ain't perfect, Daddy, but . . ."

His father chuckled and shook his head.

"I just want us to like each other." Martin's voice cracked, and he struggled to hold back the tears. Crying would ruin everything.

The room was quiet except for the TV. Scrubbing bubbles danced and sang in a bathtub. Martin stepped between his father and the TV. "What's so bad about me, Daddy?" he said.

His father moved his eyes slowly up to meet Martin's. "I've tried my best to turn you into something I could be proud of," he said.

"I want to play music, Daddy. I'm good at it. I could make you proud of me if you'd give me a—"

His father pounded his fist on the arm of the chair. "Music ain't nothing to be proud of, Martin."

"Why not?"

His father waved his hand, a look of disgust on his face. "Go on, get out of here, Martin."

"I ain't never going to be good at the things you want me to be good at," Martin said angrily. "But I got a chance of being good at what I like." His chest heaved with each breath. His pulse pounded harder inside his head.

His father jerked his head up to look at Martin, his eyes narrowed into dark slits. "If you think that violin's gonna make you something, you're dead wrong," he drawled. "You're nothing. You're—"

"You're wrong!" Martin yelled. "I ain't nothing. I may not be what you want me to be, but I ain't nothing." He took a deep breath, trying to calm his voice down. "I wish like anything I could make you like me, but I can't. But if you'd give me half a chance, I'd show you I can do something."

Martin heard the desperate tone in his voice, but he couldn't stop it. This was the first time in his life he'd ever told his feelings to his father. Maybe there was more than a snowball's chance in hell he could make him understand.

"That violin make you happy, Martin?"

"Yessir."

"That weirdo Wylene make you happy?"

"Yessir. She's my friend."

"Making a fool out of me make you happy?"

"I ain't making no fool out of you." Martin was afraid that if he stopped talking, he would never get the words out that he needed to say, so he took another deep breath and said, "I ain't playing ball no more. I don't like it. I like music. I'm going to play music."

His father jumped up so fast Martin backed up. He flinched, cowering at the same time, angry at himself for doing it.

"I won't have people laughing at me, you hear me?" His father's face was red. Suddenly he reached under the couch and pulled out the violin.

"This what you come here for, Martin?"

"Yessir."

"You think you're a musician, that it?"

"Yessir." Martin's head spun, his stomach churned. "Let me have that violin, Daddy."

Martin saw his father's mouth moving and knew he was

talking, but he couldn't hear the words because of the ringing in his ears. His father raised the violin above his head and brought it crashing down on the kitchen counter. There was an echoey thwang and then the sickening sound of splintering wood. Martin watched, numb, as the smashed body separated from the neck in one neat snap, then dangled, still attached by the strings.

It lay in a twisted pile on the linoleum floor.

It took every ounce of strength Martin had to pull his eyes away to look at his father. Calm as anything, he said, "If you think that's gonna change me, you're wrong."

Martin didn't turn to watch his father leave the trailer. He stood facing the empty space where just seconds before his father had stood. Slowly life crept back into him.

He looked at his mother, sitting on the barstool. Tears rolled down her face. Martin scooped up the crumpled heap of a violin and left. The air outside smelled sweet, like gardenias. He took a deep breath and started toward the highway, walking fast.

At Brushy Creek bridge, he stopped and looked over the rail at the water below, bubbling into sudsy pools around the rocks. A rusty can floated by, bobbing and weaving before coming to rest in the tall weeds. From a pool of still water, Martin saw his own face looking back at him and realized that he was smiling. Must have been for a long time now because his cheeks ached. He squinted at his reflection. His smile got wider when he saw how different he looked. That stranger with the knotted-up stomach and the downcast eyes was gone. Looking back was someone who knew who he was and liked what he saw. Someone looking through new eyes.

Martin cradled the violin in his arms. The beautiful wood was shattered. Splinters stuck up in every direction. Two strings had snapped and dangled from the neck. Who would have guessed that a curved piece of wood and string could have told him so much about himself?

He held the violin over the railing of the bridge and dropped it into the creek below. It hit the water with a soft slap and began to ride the slow-moving current.

It looked peaceful, floating with the leaves on top of the water. It bounced over rocks and dipped down tiny water-falls. Then it rounded the corner and disappeared.

Martin stayed on the bridge a while longer, listening to the water. Then he turned and headed back down the road, humming.

Twenty-two

WYLENE'S FACE WAS red and puffy. She made little whiny sounds and then big gaspy sounds. Piles of balled-up tissue covered the coffee table in front of her.

"I'm sorry to have to say this right to your face, Martin," she said, "but that's about the meanest thing I ever heard." She blew her nose with a loud, honking sound and shook her head. "That beautiful violin. I just can't believe it."

"I'm going to pay you back every penny," Martin said.

She flapped her hand at him and said, "Oh, for heaven's sake. I don't care about that."

"Well, I do."

Wylene took a deep breath and let it out in a puff that

blew her frizzy bangs up. "I can't imagine what would make a person do such a thing."

She went to the kitchen and ran water on a paper towel. She wiped her face, then looked at Martin and smiled. "I'm real proud of you," she said, "standing up to your daddy like that."

Martin smiled back. "I got to admit it felt pretty good, speaking my mind and all."

Wylene opened the refrigerator and peered in. "How about a BLT?"

"Naw, I got to get home."

"Aw, come on."

"Hazeline's coming." Martin got up and headed for the door. "I'm going to pay for that violin," he called back to Wylene.

"Oh, go on, get out of here," she said, and waved her hand at him.

On the way to Howard Johnson's, Martin told Hazeline what happened.

"Well, you've done crossed the Rubicon now," she said.

"What does that mean?"

"Means there's no turning back." She looked at Martin and winked. "And it's about damn time, I might add."

He put his feet on the dashboard and studied his dirty shoelaces. "You think Daddy'll ever like me?"

"Your daddy don't even like himself," she said.

"How come?"

Hazeline shook her head. "Damn if I know."

"Just because, I reckon," Martin said.

"I guess that's as good a reason as any."

When they got back to Paradise, Martin's mother was waiting on the front porch, surrounded by bulging trash bags. Hazeline gave the car horn a couple of toots and waved as she drove away.

"Let's go on and get these bottles over to the Quik Pik," his mother said. "You been letting them pile up too long."

Martin gathered up the bags and loaded them into the trunk of the car. "Sure wish I could find me a job so I wouldn't have to mess with these bottles," he said, climbing into the front seat.

His mother turned on the radio as they headed out of the trailer park. A preacher yelled to his brothers and sisters to open their hearts and let the Lord come in. The brothers and sisters hollered, "Amen!"

Suddenly Martin sat up. "Turn down there," he said, pointing to a side street. His mother turned the car quickly. "Now go down that way," Martin said. She turned again. "Now stop right up there by that mailbox."

She stopped the car and turned to Martin. "Mind telling me where we are?"

"I got to do something," he said. "It'll just take a minute, I promise."

Martin ran up to the front door. Before he could knock, Sybil came to the door.

"Is your dad here?" Martin asked.

"Well, hello to you, too." Sybil looked over Martin's shoulder at the car, raising her eyebrow.

"My mom drove me over," Martin said.

Sybil jerked her head toward the back of the house. "He's around back."

Frank Richards sat on a milk crate turning a wrench on the side of his motorcycle. When he saw Martin, he stood up and wiped his hands on a greasy rag.

"Well, hey there," he said. "Long time no see."

"I was wondering if I could ask you a favor," Martin said.

"Ask away."

"They need any help down at the gas station? Pumping gas or sweeping up or something like that?"

Frank stuffed the rag in his back pocket. "They barely got enough work for me down there, Martin." He sat down in a lawn chair and motioned for Martin to join him. "You looking for work?" He took a sip out of a coffee mug with "Life's a Bitch" painted on it.

"Yessir."

"Well now, let me think." He squinted up at the sky as if he were reading something written in the clouds.

"I can do anything," Martin said. "Maybe you got something around here." He motioned to the house. "How about the garden? I could weed and stuff."

"The garden?" Frank looked at him with twinkling eyes. "Shoot, Sybil would skin me alive if I let anybody work in that garden." He rubbed his chin thoughtfully. "But there is one thing I've been putting off for a while that I'd be pleased as punch to pay somebody to do."

"What's that?"

"See that shed over there?" He motioned to a rickety shed behind the garage. It leaned precariously to one side.

"That thing's about to bust at the seams with junk I been stuffing in there for the last two years. You want to clean that shed out?"

A car horn sounded out front. Martin looked toward the street, then back at Frank. "Yessir, I could do that no problem."

"I got to warn you, though. There's no telling what you might come across in there. Dead cat, nest of rattlesnakes. Liable to be anything in there." He took a hefty swig from his coffee mug. "Vodka and grapefruit juice," he said, as if he had read Martin's mind.

The car horn honked again.

"I can do it," Martin said.

"Okay, start whenever you're ready. Keep track of your time. I'll pay you three bucks an hour. Make a pile to keep and a pile to go. Don't throw out anything without showing me first." He smiled, and his mustache curled up. "One man's trash is another man's treasure, you know."

Mrs. Pittman's voice interrupted them. "Martin, I got to get going."

Martin looked up to see her standing at the corner of the house.

"I'm coming," he called.

His mother stared up at the colorful wall on the back of the house. Frank walked over to her.

"Every state but New Mexico and Alaska," he said

proudly. "I wish I could say I been to all them places, but I can't. Hope to someday, though."

Martin's mother smiled.

"I'm Sybil's dad," Frank said, holding out his hand.

Mrs. Pittman shook his hand and nodded. "Oh, yeah," she said. "The pickled okra."

Frank slapped Martin on the back. "Your boy here's going to be doing some work for me."

Mrs. Pittman looked at Martin, then back at Frank. "That's mighty nice of you."

"Hell, I ain't doing him no favors. He don't know what he's got himself into." He winked at Martin.

"Well," she said, looking at Martin, "we got to go. I want to get over to the flea market this afternoon."

She turned to Frank and said, "Nice meeting you," before disappearing around the side of the house.

Martin ran after her, calling over his shoulder, "I'll be back tomorrow."

Frank had given him fair warning, but Martin was still awestruck by the sight of that shed when he opened the creaky doors. Rusty tools. Bicycle wheels. A pile of bricks. A birdcage. A bent golf club. A smiling plastic Santa Claus. And more boxes than Martin had ever seen in such a small space. Boxes piled on boxes piled on boxes.

By noon the shed was nearly empty. Martin sat on a box and wiped the sweat off the back of his neck. He turned toward the house when the screen door slammed. Sybil glanced in his direction on her way out to the garden. Martin pulled his drooping socks up, brushed dust off his T-shirt, and walked over to where Sybil was picking lima beans. He held up a paper bag. "I brought you some lunch," he said.

She took the bag from him and frowned. Martin walked back toward the shed and sat in the shade, spreading his lunch out on the grass in front of him. Sybil pulled a lawn chair over and sat down. Martin nodded toward a doll lying in a rusty wagon.

"What's her name?" he said, popping a potato chip into his mouth.

When Sybil blushed, Martin quickly looked away. He stretched his legs out and tapped the toes of his sneakers together. "Sorry about the other day," he said.

Sybil took a sandwich out of the bag and held it in her lap, frowning down at Martin. He lifted his eyebrows and looked up at her through the tuft of hair that had fallen over his eyes. She set her mouth tighter and glared at him.

He watched out of the corner of his eye as she unwrapped her sandwich and took a bite. She lifted the bread and peeked inside. Her mouth twitched at the corners, then broke into a grin.

"Peanut-butter-and-banana," she said, shaking her head. Martin grinned.

"You worked things out with your dad yet?" Sybil asked.

When Martin told her about the violin, she got off the lawn chair and sat beside him on the grass. "What are you going to do now?" she said.

"Well, first I'm going to pay Wylene for the violin."

"Then what?"

"I haven't exactly figured that out yet." Martin got up and went in the shed. He grunted as he pulled out a heavy box. He wiped the dust off the top and pulled the packing tape away.

"Wow, check this out," he said, peering into the box.

Sybil looked in. "That's a saxophone."

"I know," Martin said. "Whose is it?"

"Dad's, I reckon."

"How come it's out here?"

"Who knows? He's all the time getting stuff from people when he works on their car. That's how I got my rototiller."

"Wonder what something like this costs."

Sybil shrugged. "I'm going to get us a drink."

Martin watched her walk off. When she rounded the corner, he took the saxophone out of the box. He blew the dust off it and then wiped it on his T-shirt. He glanced up to make sure Sybil was nowhere around, then put the saxophone in his mouth and pretended to play it. He leaned way back, lifting the instrument into the air the way he'd seen blues musicians on TV do it. He closed his eyes and puffed his cheeks out, lifting his fingers up and down on the keys.

When he opened his eyes, Frank was sitting on a lawn chair eating a sandwich. Martin quickly put the saxophone back in the box and disappeared into the shed. He moved boxes around noisily.

"You think I should put that in the keep pile or the go pile?" Frank called from outside the shed.

Martin clanged and banged stuff around. He carried a bent-up TV antenna out of the shed. "Depends on if you want to keep it, I guess," he said.

Frank took a bite of his sandwich. Tomato juice dripped onto his lap. "I sure ain't gonna chuck it. That thing's worth something."

"How much?"

"Hell, I don't know. It was worth a brake job to somebody over in Pickens."

"How much is a brake job?"

Frank laughed and wiped his mouth. "How much you got?"

Martin looked away and said, "I can't buy that sax. I got to pay for a violin." He looked back at Frank. "But maybe we could work a deal?"

"Now you're talking. What kind of deal?"

"Well, maybe I could trade something for it."

Frank grinned. "What've you got?"

Sybil came around the corner of the house carrying a tray with three tall glasses. She set it down on the card table. "I'm going to set up the sprinkler," she said, heading for the garden.

Martin stared out at the garden, watching Sybil stoop to pick weeds as she walked through the tall rows of corn. "I don't know. Nothing, I reckon," he said.

Frank took a long drink. His Adam's apple bobbed up and down as he swallowed. "Aw, I bet you could come up with something," he said.

"You think so?"

"Sure I do."

Martin's stomach fluttered with excitement. Maybe he could come up with something. Maybe he had nowhere to go but full steam ahead. After all, he had crossed the Rubicon.

Twenty-three

"HOW MUCH DOES a brake job cost?" Martin asked his mother.

She looked up from her paint-by-number picture. "A brake job? Lord, you're asking the wrong person." She dabbed her paintbrush in the paint and squinted at the tiny numbers on the picture. "Who needs a brake job?"

"What about a saxophone?" Martin said. "How much you think a saxophone would cost?"

His mother put the brush down and sat back on the couch. "You mind telling me what you're talking about."

Martin told her about the shed and the saxophone and the deal he could work if he only had something to trade.

"Problem is," he said, "I hadn't got anything to trade. And if I had the money to buy something to trade, then I wouldn't be needing to trade in the first place. Know what I mean?"

His mother nodded. "That's a problem, all right," she said, and went back to her painting.

Martin finished cleaning out the shed in two days. Now Frank was going to pay him extra to help haul stuff to the dump. He took one last bite of cereal before heading out the door. When he got outside, his mother was slamming down the trunk lid. She looked up at Martin and waved a bag in the air. "I got something for you," she called, grinning.

"What?"

She sat down on the steps. "Close your eyes and hold out your hand."

Martin felt the same giddy excitement he used to feel when he was little, waiting for surprises.

She put something flat and hard in his hand.

"Okay," she said.

Martin opened his eyes and looked down at the orange-and-blue license plate in his hand. Alaska, the Last Frontier.

"Hot damn!" he said.

His mother laughed.

"I got to go," Martin said. He ran to the side of the house to get his bike, then stopped and ran back to where his mother sat on the steps. He kissed her on the top of the head and said, "You're the best." He jumped on his bike, then turned to look at his mother one more time. She still sat there, smiling, and for a minute Martin thought he saw that same peaceful face he had seen on that Bible-clutching little girl on the church steps all those years ago.

When he got to the Richardses' house, he went straight around to the back, swinging the bag as he walked.

Sybil straightened up when she saw him and smiled. She rested a basket of string beans on her hip. Her broad face was tanned, her nose sprinkled with freckles. She moved toward him in that slow-motion way of hers.

"What's that?" She pointed to the bag.

"Something for your dad," Martin said. "Is he here?"

She pointed to the side of the garage. A beat-up Toyota was parked on the grass. Two skinny legs stuck out from underneath it.

"Hey, Frank," Martin called. The legs moved, and Frank emerged from under the car. He squinted up at Martin. His cheek was smudged with grease.

"Well, hey," he said. He stood up and tossed a tool into his toolbox with a clang. "What's up?"

"I came to work that deal."

"I'm game."

Martin opened the bag and took out the license plate.

"Hooeee," Frank whooped. "Sybil, would you look here?" He held it up for Sybil to see. The three of them stood there, beaming at one another. Martin thought about that day he had looked back at Sybil and Frank standing in the garden and had felt like an outsider. Now here he was standing with them. On the inside.

It was Frank who broke the spell. He went to the shed and came back with the saxophone.

"It's all yours, buddy," he said.

Martin took the saxophone and ran his fingers over the little dents on the side.

"Did Beethoven ever play the saxophone?" Sybil asked.

Martin laughed. "I doubt it," he said, "but I bet he could have."

He looked down at the saxophone. "Mind if I leave my bike here?"

Sybil shook her head. Martin put the saxophone in his mouth and blew. A puff of dust shot out the end. They all laughed. Martin blew again. A low, hoarse sound came out.

Martin started walking slowly toward the street. He held the saxophone to his lips and blew. The saxophone squawked. The squawk got louder.

Martin kept walking and blowing, squeaking and squawking, down the road and over the Rubicon toward Paradise.